"Able Team is taking on home base!"

"Looks like they're winning, too," Bolan remarked grimly.

"I don't believe this," Grimaldi said. "They're killing our own people down there!"

The Jeep pulled up to the front door of the main house. Lyons and Schwarz jumped from the rig and raced to the door. An access code was needed to get inside, but Able knew it and the variation number used when the place faced a crisis situation. The door opened and the commandos entered.

"We have to get down there and stop them."

"God, Sarge," the pilot stated. "You don't think we'll have to kill them...."

"I said stop them," the Executioner replied, "and I mean any way that's necessary, Jack."

MACK BOLAN ®
The Executioner

DON PENDLETON'S
THE EXECUTIONER®
VIRTUAL DESTRUCTION

A GOLD EAGLE BOOK FROM
WORLDWIDE®

TORONTO • NEW YORK • LONDON
AMSTERDAM • PARIS • SYDNEY • HAMBURG
STOCKHOLM • ATHENS • TOKYO • MILAN
MADRID • WARSAW • BUDAPEST • AUCKLAND

First edition May 1999
ISBN 0-373-64245-8

Special thanks and acknowledgment to
William Fieldhouse for his contribution to this work.

VIRTUAL DESTRUCTION

Printed in U.S.A.

By knowing things that exist, you can know that which does not exist.

—Miyamoto Musashi
A Book of Five Rings

Everyone practices propaganda—from neighborhood gossip to sophisticated mind control. Control an individual's perception of reality and you control the individual. This form of manipulation can be as dangerous as any military weapon.

—Mack Bolan

THE
MACK BOLAN®
LEGEND

Nothing less than a war could have fashioned the destiny of the man called Mack Bolan. Bolan earned the Executioner title in the jungle hell of Vietnam.

But this soldier also wore another name—Sergeant Mercy. He was so tagged because of the compassion he showed to wounded comrades-in-arms and Vietnamese civilians.

Mack Bolan's second tour of duty ended prematurely when he was given emergency leave to return home and bury his family, victims of the Mob. Then he declared a one-man war against the Mafia.

He confronted the Families head-on from coast to coast, and soon a hope of victory began to appear. But Bolan had broken society's every rule. That same society started gunning for this elusive warrior—to no avail.

So Bolan was offered amnesty to work within the system against terrorism. This time, as an employee of Uncle Sam, Bolan became Colonel John Phoenix. With a command center at Stony Man Farm in Virginia, he and his new allies—Able Team and Phoenix Force—waged relentless war on a new adversary: the KGB.

But when his one true love, April Rose, died at the hands of the Soviet terror machine, Bolan severed all ties with Establishment authority.

Now, after a lengthy lone-wolf struggle and much soul-searching, the Executioner has agreed to enter an "arm's-length" alliance with his government once more, reserving the right to pursue personal missions in his Everlasting War.

1

The wind howled from the north. It seemed to express an angry protest that humans had intruded in a wilderness located far from the cities of Fairbanks and Anchorage. The Brooks Range wasn't hospitable to man. Perhaps nature didn't object to a few Inuit and Aleuts in the area, but it didn't make their survival easy and the original people of Alaska used only what their simple traditional life-style required. They didn't gouge into the natural resources like the industrial gluttons who valued profits above the ecology.

Mack Bolan hadn't come to the Brooks Range to harm the environment or plunder its resources. Ironically, the enemy he stalked called themselves the Commandos for Mother Earth and claimed to be devoted to the protection of the environment and the Alaskan wilderness. Their tactics caused a fair amount of misery for the oil companies operating in the region. But Bolan doubted their motives. The CME saboteurs didn't help the environment by blowing up parts of the pipeline to spill hundreds of tons of oil across the land they claimed they fought for.

The Executioner didn't receive any special consideration for his good intentions. The hostile environment presented him with ample challenge as he sat inside the small tent and ate cold rations with little pleasure. His compact heater-stove had shorted-out during the night. Without heat or a source to cook food or boil water for coffee, his watch promised to be very uncomfortable in the subzero weather.

Of course, he wore a heavy winter parka and other cold weather gear. The bulky field pants, arctic boots and gloves were unfamiliar attire. He felt weighted down and restricted by the protective bundle of clothing. Bolan hoped any human opponents he encountered would face similar problems that reduced rapid movement. The Kevlar body armor under his parka might help him survive a gun battle, but he knew the term bulletproof was relative at best. One was never really safe when assaulted by high-velocity projectiles.

He finished his meal and turned his attention to his own arsenal of weapons for the occasion. A Beretta 93-R was in its usual position under his left arm, carried in a special holster designed to accommodate a sound suppressor attached to the barrel. The pistol was a formidable piece of hardware in the hands of a marksman, and was equipped with a selector switch that included 3-round full-auto bursts. Fully loaded with hollowpoint 9 mm Parabellum rounds, the Beretta was ready when the Executioner went to war.

An Israeli-made Desert Eagle rode in a holster on Bolan's hip. Despite the name, the Eagle would function admirably in a cold climate and the mighty .44 Magnum cartridge could bring down any two-legged opponent...even a hungry polar bear, which was a legitimate concern in the area. However, due to the climate, Bolan carried it in an unfamiliar button-flap holster to protect it from the cold and snow. He wouldn't be able to draw either pistol rapidly.

The Executioner also had a primary assault weapon

for the occasion. He selected a Fusil Automatique Légère, better known as an FAL. Manufactured by the Fabrique Nationale Herstal—FN—the FAL was one of the Belgian arms designer's most successful and respected products. The FAL was larger and heavier than the M-16 he generally favored, so Bolan reckoned the weapon was better suited for the Alaskan climate. The M-16 was more apt to freeze-up in cold weather or jam if snow seeped into the receiver. Some might argue that opinion, but Bolan based it on his own experience.

The FAL also fired 7.62 mm cartridge rather than the smaller M-16 5.56 mm round. He assumed any enemies he encountered would be bundled in thick protective garb. A bullet with more force was better for the situation.

Bolan also had grenades and extra magazines of ammo, as well as fighting knives and wire garrotes. He wasn't certain how well armed the CME terrorists might be, but he intended to be at least as well prepared for combat as the enemy. The soldier had also included Starlite night-vision goggles and a scope mount for the FAL. A radio transceiver allowed him to keep contact with rangers on patrol in the area and oil company security personnel involved with the protection of the pipelines. A snowmobile was hidden under a white tarp by a snowbank sixty-five yards from Bolan's position if he needed transportation.

The Executioner intended to tough out the night without the heater. He had endured worse hardships during previous missions, and it would be worth the discomfort if he could nail the terrorists. He had spent most of three days at the lonely, chilly station in hope of catching the enemy in the act.

Sabotage of oil pipelines wasn't the sort of terrorism

generally handled by the Executioner. Oil companies didn't rank very high on Bolan's list of sympathetic organizations. Until other forms of energy replaced petroleum, these companies might be necessary. Yet, they were extremely wealthy, more than able to protect themselves from vandals, fanatics and occasional lunatics. Of course, the Commandos for Mother Earth were no more sympathetic, in Bolan's opinion, and the more he learned about them the worse they appeared. Their tactics were ruthless and destructive. CME was also attempting to blackmail the petroleum companies with demands for sixty million dollars to cease the attacks on the pipelines. Apparently, the terrorists' real motive had more to do with monetary gain than the ecology.

The cybernetics team at Stony Man Farm continued to gather information about the situation as a potential mission for the elite enforcement organization. The mainframe had taps to thousands of other computer systems that ranged from NSA, CIA and Interpol to local police, DMV offices and credit-card companies. A high-tech search for data and evaluation of evidence discovered a new resident in Fairbanks had recently acquired an Alaska driver's license, applied for several credit cards and opened accounts in three banks. The name used was bogus, but the face and description of Charles Attwill belonged to Peter Anthony DiCarlo.

Bolan recognized the name. The DiCarlo brothers had been subcapos for a Mob operation in Trenton, New Jersey. The Executioner had personally put them out of business and killed the elder brother, Salvador DiCarlo, along with a number of button men on the payroll. Peter had vanished...until now.

A made man, the middle-level Mob boss from Jersey

wasn't likely to head for Alaska because he wanted a change of scenery. Especially not a greedy, cold-blooded gangster like DiCarlo. He had been involved with the usual syndicate business in Trenton, but DiCarlo had carried out some blackmail schemes along with the narcotics trafficking, protection rackets and loan-shark operations. Bolan figured DiCarlo had conjured up the Commandos for Mother Earth scheme as a cover for an old-fashioned shakedown.

The Executioner knew some big coincidences occur, but he was positive DiCarlo was connected with an effort to extort sixty million dollars from the Alaskan oil companies. The Commandos of Mother Earth was another story. Bolan believed the CME consisted of a band of killers and hoods trained in fundamental demolitions led by DiCarlo. They seemed to be ecoterrorists, attempting to blackmail the oil companies. A demand for sixty million dollars would be one hell of a prize. Enough to finance DiCarlo's criminal operations for any illegal enterprise he might fancy in the future.

Bolan was sure his theory was correct, but he still needed to put to rest that lingering doubt before he could nail DiCarlo. The capo seemed to be keeping his nose clean. Aside from using a fake name and background, DiCarlo hadn't done anything to suggest he was involved with the CME. Bolan needed to catch the terrorists in the act.

To do this, he had staked out a section of pipe that was a tempting target for the enemy. It would be easy to sabotage the seams of a huge metal bolt that connected two massive pipes. The area was isolated, many miles from the nearest town or oil station patrolled by company security. Yet, a lonely road was close enough to offer a clear path to and from the site. Bolan knew the attitudes and prejudices of a typical Mob guy. DiCarlo would probably regard anyone not born and raised in a major city as a dim-witted hick. He preferred a hood involved in a life of crime since childhood and who'd spent at least a year in prison.

City boys favored roads rather than traveling across the deep snow, and they'd be more afraid of encountering a bear or pack of wolves than human opponents. They'd probably have a local guide to help them find the spot, but a street soldier would certainly be in command of the team.

Stony Man Farm provided Bolan with ID as a special agent with the Department of Justice named Michael Belasko and even programmed the information into government computers. The knowledge and skill of the Farm's cybernetic team allowed this sort of subterfuge to go undetected. Belasko had the highest authority behind him. Stony Man could even acquire support from the President of the United States—the only person fully aware of the full scope of the organization.

Thanks to this apparent special status, Bolan got full cooperation from the security personnel employed by the Watley Petroleum Corporation as well as forest rangers in the area. He had arranged for them to increase patrols at other sections of the pipeline that might appeal to the CME. Of course, they couldn't be sure the plan would work. If the enemy didn't go for the bait, the Executioner would try something else.

MOVEMENT ALONG A RIDGE near the pipeline drew Bolan's attention. Figures bundled in cold weather gear shuffled through the snow from the direction of the road roughly five hundred yards from the site. They seemed clumsy, unfamiliar with the terrain. Bolan guessed they were city boys out of their element. They were clad in forest-camouflage parkas, better suited for deer hunting than blending with the snowbound tundra environment.

Five men, Bolan observed. One carried a bolt-action rifle with a scope. Probably the local guide, he guessed. Two packed pump-action shotguns, and another had a submachine gun that resembled a British L-2 A-3 Sterling—most likely a Canadian 9 mm C-1 subgun. The last member of the group carried a small duffel bag slung over one shoulder and a compact MAC-10 machine pistol over the other.

Bolan wrapped the barrel and frame of his FAL rifle with a white cloth as he watched the men approach the pipeline. The assault weapon appeared to be bound with a bandage, camouflaged to blend with the snow and Bolan's white parka. He took a small, yet powerful radio receiver with an amplifier speaker from his gear, and slipped a throat microphone around his neck. The Executioner left his shelter and headed downhill toward the pipes.

He had practiced his descent during his days stationed at the site and knew the best route to take. Concealed by mounds of snow, the intruders wouldn't see the soldier as he waded through knee-deep drifts to the foot of the hill. Bolan paused to set the receiver-speaker unit into the hollow of a fallen log before he completed his trek to a row of small pine trees. They provided good cover and a clear view of the pipeline approximately three hundred yards from his new position.

The men drew closer to the oil pipes. The guy with the bag unslung his bundle as the others stood guard and glanced about with obvious apprehension. Bolan realized the bag contained explosives and the demolitions man was about to sabotage the pipeline. He had

enough proof, and he didn't want to give the man
enough time to prepare the blasting caps or detonators.
That would add an extra hazard to an already dangerous
situation.

Bolan pressed a switch to activate the throat mike.
He barely needed to speak above a whisper to transmit
to the receiver unit. The soldier adopted a prone stance
in the snow, set the butt of his rifle to his shoulder and
placed a gloved hand by the trigger with the index finger ready.

"Stand where you are and don't move!" Bolan ordered. "Throw down your weapons and that bag!"

His voice boomed from the speaker on the hill, ech-
oing into the woods. The five men swung weapons toward the general direction of the voice. The demo man
dumped his bag only to grab his Ingram chopper with
both gloved hands. None of the gunners pointed a barrel close to Bolan's true position.

"I said drop the hardware!"

The thug with the C-1 subgun opened fire, spraying
the hill with a burst of 9 mm slugs. Snow splattered
from the wild salvo. The man with the bolt rifle
dropped to a kneeling stance and tried to find Bolan
through the telescope. He presented the greatest threat
at the moment, although he continued to look for Bolan
on the hill.

The Executioner switched the FAL to semiauto and
aimed with care. He squeezed the trigger. A 7.62 mm
round hit the rifleman in the side of the head, shattering
bone, and spewing blood and brains across the snow
near the others. They jumped back; cursing as the
corpse slumped to the ground. One of the shotgunners
slipped and fell backward, triggering his weapon and

unleashing a burst of 12-gauge pellets into the night sky.

This startled the others into a blind response of desperate gunfire at the hillside. More snow sprayed from the assault of bullets and buckshots.

Bolan selected the next target. Although the demo man's short-range MAC-10 didn't present an immediate threat, the bundle of explosives could still be used to attack the pipeline if he could reach it.

The Executioner took out the risk with a single shot from the FAL. The bullet drilled the demolitions man in the chest, just left of the breastbone. A 7.62 mm heart attack brought the hoodlum down. His body twitched in the snow as one of his comrades realized Bolan's true position. The guy had to have noticed the muzzle-flash of the FAL. He swung his shotgun toward the pine trees and opened fire.

Bolan watched buckshot tear into the snow about 150 yards from his position. He was well out of range, and the C-1 couldn't reach him at his present distance either. However, the man with the chopper made the mistake of reaching for the demo bag. Bolan fired another 7.62 mm round into his upper torso. The guy stood staring at the crimson stain on his parka as if surprised by the mortal wound. Bolan hit him with a second round, convincing the hood he was dead. The body landed on the blood-smeared snow between the other two corpses.

Only two hoods remained, and they decided they couldn't fight Bolan's marksmanship with their short-range shotguns. The pair bolted and awkwardly ran in the direction of the road. The Executioner could have easily shot them both in the back as they fled, but he held his fire. Bolan didn't kill unless he had to, and it wasn't necessary at the moment.

The soldier rose and followed his quarry, trudging through the snow at a steady pace. The drifts were too dense to run, and he knew the thugs would only exhaust themselves if they attempted to gallop for the road. Bolan switched the FAL to full-auto and took aim once more.

A trio of 7.62 mm slugs ripped globs of icy snow from the top of a mound less than a yard from the pair. The warning caused the hoods to stop in midstride. One turned and fired his shotgun at the tall white-clad figure that stalked them. Bolan remained out of range of the buckshot and merely watched as a hail of pellets descended into the snow in front of him.

"Last chance," Bolan announced. "Throw down the guns and give up or you know what happens."

The guy tossed his pump gun aside but immediately reached inside his parka and drew a revolver from shoulder leather. Bolan triggered a 3-round burst before the hood could attempt to point his handgun. Projectiles sliced through the gunner's face. The man's knees buckled as he raised a gloved hand to his pulverized features. Fingers touched the scarlet mass that had been a face. Then the corpse toppled into the snow.

"Shit!" the last man exclaimed. "I quit!"

He had discarded his shotgun and thrust both arms high. The thug's hands were empty, his face pale and eyes wide with terror. Bolan planted the butt of his FAL rifle on his hip as he moved closer, barrel still pointed at the enemy gunman.

"DiCarlo didn't clear this with the Family back in Jersey," Bolan announced. "They're not too happy with him for pulling this stunt. Bad for business."

"Hey," the thug began, "I was just doin' my job! Capo tells us to blow up the goddamn pipelines, so we do it! Ain't that what we're supposed to do? Follow orders? Right?"

"That excuse didn't work for the Nazis," the Executioner said. "Maybe your lawyer will help you come up with a better story before you go to court."

The guy's jaw dropped, and he glared at Bolan with astonishment and anger. "You mean you're a cop?" he demanded.

"No. I'm just the guy who will blow your head off if you give me any trouble. Let's go call the cops. Rangers are the closest law enforcement in the area."

"You're as good as dead," the hood stated.

"Yeah?" Bolan said, unimpressed. "I don't know how many times I've heard that before, and I'm still here. Move it."

He marched the thug toward the trees near the shoulder of the road. A Jeep was parked there, and Bolan figured the vehicle would help the rangers find the area. He told the captive to hug a tree. The guy looked at Bolan as if he thought the soldier were nuts.

"A tree?" he asked.

"That one," Bolan explained and pointed at his choice. "The trunk isn't too big for you to get your arms around it."

"Crazy bastard," the hood complained, but he obeyed the instructions.

Bolan produced a pair of steel handcuffs and snapped them on the man's wrists. The guy wouldn't be going anywhere unless he could uproot the tree or tear off one of his own hands to escape. Bolan left him cuffed, the trunk between his arms and the getaway car less than ten yards away.

The Executioner headed back to the hill and his tent. He knelt by the transceiver and switched on the radio to contact the rangers. A transmission came through before he could raise the mike.

"Snow Hawk," a voice declared. "This is Watley HQ. Do you read me? Over."

Bolan keyed the mike. "Snow Hawk here. Read you. Over."

"Jesus, Snow Hawk! Where the hell have you been? We've been trying to contact you for almost an hour."

"I've been busy taking care of your CME problem," Bolan explained. "You want to get off this frequency so I can call the rangers and have them take care of what's left here?"

"I...I still think you'd better get back here, Snow Hawk. Something terrible has happened."

"They hit another section of pipe?" Bolan asked.

"No," the voice replied. "Graham Sutton arrived here by helicopter. He's the vice president of Watley Petroleum."

"That's nice," Bolan said with a sigh.

"You don't understand. He's been murdered!"

2

The Watley Petroleum Station was virtually a small city erected near the coast of the Arctic Ocean. Dominated by the great metal towers of the oil derricks and huge storage tanks, other structures had been added as the complex increased in size. Crude barracks had been replaced by reinforced apartment buildings that housed the Watley employees in comfort. A hydroelectric generator system produced power for the station. Lights cast a harsh glare on the domed buildings, the maze of thick pipelines and the derricks.

Mack Bolan arrived on his snowmobile. Guards acknowledged his Justice ID and opened the gate. Alex Hanson met Bolan at the entrance. The Executioner recognized the deputy chief of security. Tall, lean and grim, Hanson would have made an outstanding funeral director. He seemed even more somber than usual when he greeted the soldier. Neither man said more than half a dozen words until they climbed into the back of a shuttle limo. Hanson glanced at the duffel bags and weapons Bolan had placed on the floor.

"You said the Commandos for Mother Earth are no longer a problem?" the security man inquired.

"I've got to make one more visit to finish it off," Bolan assured him. "The pipelines won't be targeted by CME anymore. Rangers have a live terrorist in custody, and the FBI office at Fairbanks will soon have the fingerprints and dental X rays of the four dead men.''

''You killed them?'' Hanson asked with surprise.

''They didn't die from frostbite,'' the Executioner replied. ''So what happened to the Watley vice president? You told me he'd been murdered, but no other details.''

''I was worried about security on the radio,'' Hanson explained. ''The other oil companies in the area monitor various wavelengths trying to steal information. Industrial espionage is a serious problem.''

''I'm sure it is, but I didn't come here to help you guys keep secrets from the competition. The murdered VP was named Sutton?''

Hanson nodded. The limo rolled across the well-plowed surface and headed for a side wing of the main office building, where Bolan knew the security center was located. He guessed Hanson would deliver him to his boss, Chief of Security Paul Greely.

''Graham Sutton landed on the chopper pad,'' Hanson began at last. ''You can see the helicopter is still there. He entered the building with his assistant, a secretary or accountant or something like that, and two personal bodyguards. Mr. Baker and I were among the reception group to greet him. Then Paul approached along with our lead engineer and science chief. Suddenly, Paul screamed, drew his gun and started shooting.''

''Paul?'' Bolan asked with surprise. ''You mean Paul Greely? You mean your boss, the head of security here, opened fire on the vice president of Watley Oil?''

Hanson nodded as he spoke. ''He pumped two .45 slugs into Sutton before anybody could react. I was so stunned I just stood there. The bodyguards went for their guns, and Paul managed to nail one of them before the other guy shot back.''

"Is Greeley dead?"

"The bodyguard hit him in the stomach with a couple rounds, but Paul was still alive. He lay on his back, .45 Colt still in his fist, and he didn't try to shoot at us. Used the gun on himself instead. Stuck the barrel in his mouth and blew his brains out. Worse goddamn thing I ever saw, Belasko."

"Any idea why he did it?"

"Well, I've heard taking a bullet in the stomach is awful painful. Maybe he killed himself to end his suffering."

"I mean why did he shoot Sutton?"

"Jesus," Hanson began. "I can't even guess why. Must have just gone crazy. Paul didn't have anything against Sutton. Never met the man before. I knew Paul for five years and never heard him say anything against Sutton or any other executive with Watley. He always seemed like a sane and rational guy. I wouldn't believe this happened if I hadn't been there to see it myself."

Bolan opened his parka and pushed the hood back. The limo was warm, and he knew the building was well heated. He considered what Hanson had told him before he spoke.

"I'll contact Justice and make sure they handle a detailed investigation. That's about all I can do, Hanson."

"You won't do it yourself?" the security man asked with disappointment. "You're supposed to be a hotshot federal troubleshooter."

"I just came back from shooting trouble in the snow," Bolan explained. "My work here is almost finished. In fact I don't really have anything left to do at this site except return the snowmobile I borrowed."

"You're not even going to look at the bodies of Paul, Sutton and the dead bodyguard?"

"I've seen a lot of bodies. Too many. Not much I can tell about why a man flips out and kills a total stranger. Maybe a medical examiner will find a brain tumor or some sort of chemical imbalance to offer an explanation. Sorry, Hanson. This sort of thing just isn't my field."

"Guess not," Hanson replied with a sigh. "Well, I'd say you did accomplish your job, and the company is very thankful. I might not sound too happy right now. This has come as quite a shock."

"Yeah, I understand that. Can you get a chopper ready to fly me to Fairbanks?"

"Sure," Hanson said. "When will you need it?"

"Soon as possible. I want to catch the leader of the Commandos for Mother Earth before he realizes his plan has gone wrong and decides to go on the run again."

"Again? You know the guy?"

"I know about him," Bolan explained. "We've never met, but I'll introduce myself when I catch up with him."

PETER DiCARLO STUCK the computer disks into a leather pocket inside the lid of his briefcase. He would need the information and records stored on the floppies. DiCarlo had deliberately used a simple home computer model because he was unfamiliar with such machines and didn't want anything complicated. It had been used only for records of his business as a sort of high-tech filing system. DiCarlo couldn't access information from other computers, but no sneaky mainframe of a federal agency could tap into his isolated machine, either.

He piled the "Charles Attwill" identification items on the bed beside the case. Driver's license, credit cards, none of it could be used if his men in the field had been caught sabotaging the pipeline. He would also have to leave more than a hundred grand in a bank account under that name. DiCarlo would assume a new identity with another fake passport, social security card and other documentation.

Vince Grasso stared at the closet, unsure what to pack in a suitcase for his boss. The man didn't want to anger his capo. DiCarlo usually had good control of his temper, but he was already upset and would be more likely to explode. The young mobster still kept in shape, and he had been a top Golden Gloves contender as a kid in Jersey. Grasso would usually take care of a fistfighter with a bullet, but he couldn't shoot his boss or even hit back if DiCarlo decided to use him for a punching bag.

"You got a lot of nice clothes here, Mr. Attwill," Grasso began. "The Italian suits and shoes must be expensive."

"I don't give a damn, Vinny!" DiCarlo snapped. "Grab one goddamn suit and a pair of dress shoes, pack them and leave the rest. I got more important things to think about right now."

"Yes, sir, Mr. Attwill…I mean…"

"Better stop calling me that," the capo ordered. "Gotta dump that ID. Just call me Pete for now."

"Okay," Grasso agreed as he pulled a suit from the closet.

"Leave the blue one," DiCarlo told him. "Get the double-breasted pinstripe and the silk shirts."

"Right," Grasso replied as he followed the instructions. "How about these shoes, Boss...Pete?"

"Brown shoes with a black-and-white pinstripe?" DiCarlo said with disgust. "What the hell? You color-blind, Vinny? Pack the black pair. And don't pack the white necktie. With the pinstripe, it'll make me look like a gangster. Not the kind of image I need right now."

Grasso nodded and packed the items in the case while DiCarlo turned his attention to the more vital matters of his new identity and escape. He would burn his Attwill ID and flush it down the toilet. Joey Parvo was in the bathroom again. The guy had weak kidneys and seemed to be in the john all the time. He'd better hurry up, DiCarlo thought. When something went wrong everything else seemed to happen too....

There was a knock at the door. DiCarlo's spine stiffened and his stomach knotted. Where the hell was his gun? The drawer of the nightstand, he recalled. DiCarlo seldom left his apartment since he arrived in Fairbanks. Too cold outside. His triggerman packed heat, so he seldom carried a gun.

"Probably Lou," Grasso commented with a shrug.

The thug didn't seem concerned the cops or the Feds might be at the door. Maybe he didn't realize how serious the situation was since the men in the field hadn't reported back to DiCarlo. Hopefully, Luigi "Lou" Damilano was at the door. DiCarlo had sent him out to make some phone calls and swap the plates on the cars. DiCarlo's phone might be tapped, and he didn't want to take any chances...not even to find out when the next train or bus would leave for Anchorage.

"Make sure before you open the door," DiCarlo insisted.

Grasso left the bedroom and headed through the narrow hall to the front room. He heard DiCarlo's voice shout at Joey to get his ass out of the bathroom. The capo was too worried about the Feds, Grasso thought. Maybe they had nailed the guys sent out to sabotage the pipelines, but none of them would have broken and ratted out DiCarlo in such a short time. They would have insisted on lawyers and called a mouthpiece on the Mob payroll. Grasso figured they still had at least two days before the law would come for them. By then they would be either in Canada or back in the main forty-eight states.

The thug strode through the luxury apartment and headed for the door. He would be glad to get the hell out of Alaska. The weather sucked. Grasso hoped they'd settle in California next. At least they'd be warm all year.

He reached for the .357 snub-nosed pistol in a cross-draw holster with one hand as he leaned to the peephole in the door. Grasso saw the thin face and droopy dark eyes of Lou Damilano. The lens to the peephole distorted Damilano's features and seemed to stretch them to caricature proportions. Grasso unlocked the dead bolt and opened the door.

Damilano hurled across the threshold, slamming into Grasso. Both men staggered across the living room. Grasso glimpsed a shape behind the Mob button man and realized something had to have shoved Damilano and used him as a battering ram to enter. The guy was still pressed against him, but Grasso reached for his gun. His friend's head thrust forward and butted Grasso in the mouth.

The mobster tasted blood. The son of a bitch behind Lou had to have grabbed Damilano by the back of the head and forced the skull into Grasso's face. Suddenly, the invader appeared next to Damilano—a big guy with dark hair, hard blue eyes and a fancy pistol in his fist. The gun became a blur as it smashed into Grasso's jaw. The hood dropped to the carpet, unconscious before he hit the floor.

The Executioner had already scanned the room for opponents but glanced about again, Beretta 93-R held ready. Damilano stood on unsteady legs, forehead gashed by Grasso's front teeth. Bolan had cuffed the guy's hands behind his back when he caught him in the hall. It had been easy enough to march the hardman to the door so his face would be on display at the peephole.

The Executioner rammed an elbow into Damilano's solar plexus. The thug doubled over, gasping, and Bolan clipped him behind the ear with the butt of his Beretta, dropping Damilano to the floor next to Grasso. The soldier knelt by the senseless hoodlums. He had previously relieved Damilano of a .38 Smith & Wesson pistol. A quick frisk confirmed that Grasso carried only the .357 and no backup piece or hidden knife. With one hand, Bolan thumbed the cylinder catch, swung open the wheel gun and ejected the Magnum shells from the chambers.

"Vinny? Lou?" a voice called from another room.

"Yeah," Bolan replied.

He moved to a sofa and jammed the empty revolver behind the cushion, out of sight and out of immediate reach of any potential opponent. Expensive leather sofa, Bolan noticed. All of the furniture in DiCarlo's apartment had cost a lot of money. Everything was large and flashy, typical for a street hood who made good and needed to have the trappings of wealth around to reassure himself that he had come a long way from the gutter. A wide-screen television set, complex stereo system and a well-stocked bar added to the creature comforts.

A figure approached. Bolan saw a shadow and readied his pistol before Peter DiCarlo stepped into view. The capo held a briefcase in one hand, the other on the butt of a compact .380 autoloader stuck in his belt. He failed to see Bolan until the soldier spoke.

"I'll blow your head off if you try to draw that gun," he warned. "I heard you were always better with your fists than a piece anyway."

DiCarlo stared at him with astonishment.

"Who the hell are you?"

"I have the drop on you, and that's all you need to know. Use your thumb and little finger to ease that gun out, and drop it on the floor. Don't do anything to make me nervous, Pete. This Beretta has a hair trigger, and it won't take much to set it off."

DiCarlo slowly obeyed the instructions. He seemed more surprised than frightened as he studied the stranger. Bolan had changed to his familiar black combat gear and boots, which allowed greater movement. He carried only the 93-R for the visit, but figured that would be enough.

"You don't look like a cop," DiCarlo commented. "Sure as hell not a Fed. Who you working for, fella?"

"Kick that gun over here," Bolan ordered.

"Okay," the thug agreed. "You know who I am. Bet I can pay you better than whoever sent you."

"I don't have a price tag, Pete," Bolan stated. "Drop the case. You're not going anywhere until the cops come for you."

"So you're not a cop."

"They can have the collar. Knowing you're finished and about to go to prison for the rest of your life will be all the reward I need."

"What am I being accused of? You're not reading me my rights or showing me a badge or anything else."

"You know what this is about, Don Pete. They have enough evidence to fry you already, and there's probably more in that case. I told you to drop it. If you don't, I'll figure you're up to something, and I'll have to put a 9 mm through your kneecap for making me nervous."

Suddenly, a shape charged from the bedroom corridor. Joey Parvo had finished his business in the bathroom and heard enough to realize his boss was in trouble. The henchman rushed into the living room, a revolver in his fist.

Parvo was basically a dumb brute, and his tactics fitted his limited mental level. Yet, he might have succeeded against a less experienced and untrained opponent. Unfortunately for Parvo, Mack Bolan was the ultimate professional warrior. Reflexes and skill acted faster than conscious thought. Bolan swung the Beretta toward the new threat and opened fire. Parvo was a large target, easy to hit at close range. The 93-R snarled a short 3-round burst. Nine millimeter Parabellum rounds chopped a vicious column of bloodied holes from the point of his chin to the crown of his forehead.

The thug collapsed, dead before he could trigger his own weapon. However, the split second required for Bolan to take down the attacker presented Pete DiCarlo with the opportunity he had hoped for. The capo hurled the briefcase at Bolan's extended arm. It struck the soldier's wrist, jarring the Beretta from his grasp. The

93-R hurled across the room as DiCarlo lunged at Bolan.

DiCarlo relied on his boxing background and launched a left jab. The fist hit Bolan hard to the right of his sternum and knocked him back two steps. DiCarlo immediately followed with a right cross for the classic "one-two" that had put many opponents on their backs.

The Executioner's left hand rose to swipe a palm into the attacker's arm as he weaved away from the punch. This increased DiCarlo's own momentum and nearly threw him off balance. Bolan whirled with the swing of his arm to make a rapid clockwise turn and ducked low to lash out with his right forearm. He caught his adversary behind the knee, buckling the leg. As Bolan rose, he scooped the leg high. DiCarlo had already pushed his weight into this leg to try to compensate for the punch he missed to maintain balance. The unexpected tactic lifted the hood's left foot from the floor as well, sending him crashing hard on his back.

Bolan didn't give his opponent a chance to recover. He swung his boot and slammed the heel into DiCarlo's face. The guy's head bounced from the kick, and he sprawled unconscious on the floor, an ugly welt marking the blow to his cheek. The Executioner grunted with satisfaction and looked for his gun.

The sound of shoe leather on the carpet warned Bolan an instant before another attack came from the rear. Strong hands grabbed the soldier's jacket at the shoulders. The man behind him shoved, attempting to drive Bolan into a wall, window or furniture, hoping to smash the fight from him. It was a standard street-fighting tactic that usually worked fairly well.

Bolan dropped to one knee and ducked his head.

Once more, his opponent's own momentum worked against him. Vince Grasso's body hurled over Bolan's crouched form. The thug lost his grip on the Executioner's coat and sailed into the entertainment center. At least two thousand dollars' worth of stereo equipment and CDs crashed to the floor with the stunned mobster.

"Nice try," the Executioner admitted as he gazed down at his fallen opponent. "Want to go again?"

Grasso looked up at Bolan with glazed eyes. He didn't utter a response because his jaw had already been broken when the Executioner slammed him with the Beretta. The guy was tough and had proved it by still making a move on the formidable stranger, but Grasso had collected some more bruises and cuts from the second crash landing. He managed a weak head shake to confirm he'd had enough.

"Wise decision," Bolan stated.

He located his Beretta and glanced at his wristwatch. The cops would arrive in another minute or so, and he could let them take over. The Executioner estimated he'd be headed back to Stony Man Farm by 1800 hours.

3

Carl Lyons saw something move and swung his weapon toward the simulated brick wall. The training pistol felt remarkably similar to the Colt Python he favored. The weight and grip were roughly the same, although the special gloves he wore seemed awkward.

A shape bolted from the edge of the wall. Lyons's finger didn't squeeze the trigger when he saw the four-legged figure. The dog looked real. It didn't move in the jerky, cartoon-style of most computer simulations. The dog appeared to be a German shepherd, about medium size, with brown-and-black markings natural in tone.

Lyons was impressed by the quality of the image, but he didn't allow his eyes to remain on the dog. The computer program had probably displayed the animal to catch him off guard. An "opponent" was likely to appear by the wall.

The crash of glass drew his attention to a window. A human shape appeared at the broken pane behind the barrel and frame of a weapon. Damn gun looked real. Lyons reacted immediately, moving for cover and snap aiming his pistol. The enemy weapon fired. No laser lights streaked from the gun. The muzzle-flash and report of the weapon proved realistic enough to send a lance of fear along Lyons's spine. He triggered the pistol, and the hefty recoil surprised him. The weapon kicked as hard as a real .357 Magnum pistol.

A scream seemed to come from above. Lyons saw the figure at the window turn sharply and drop from view. The kill looked real. Lyons didn't feel as if he had shot a cardboard image at a simulated combat range or zapped a computer bad guy. His astonishment threatened to distract him, but Lyons's survival instincts caused him to glance about for his next opponent.

He scanned the windows. A typical program might conjure up more enemy gunmen at the windows and mix in an occasional civilian hostage or good guy image dressed in a police uniform to try to catch Lyons off guard. He'd lose points by shooting a noncombatant. Something like that wasn't likely to occur in a real combat situation, but the game masters loved that sort of crap. However, no figures popped up at the windows.

Lyons headed for a door. The soles of his boots seemed to impact with a sidewalk that didn't exist. He glanced about for possible danger as he reached the door. He saw no one at the windows or the edges of the building, but he didn't know what was on the other side of the door. It could be booby-trapped or a gunman might be hidden there.

Circumstances and available equipment limited his choice of action. He moved away from the door, placed his back to the wall and aimed the pistol. Lyons fired two rounds into the doorframe near the knob. The dull ring of metal on metal sounded amid the roar of the weapon. Lyons saw the door open, the frame splinter and the mangled remnants of a broken lock drop to the pavement. He slowly approached. An arm swung around the edge of the door, a blue-black handgun in a fist. Lyons fired a round into the panel roughly six inches to the right of the arm. A shape tumbled from behind the door. He glanced down at the image of a man on the floor. It twitched slightly, then lay still. The face was covered by crimson and gray globs that resembled chunks of brain matter.

"Jesus," Lyons muttered.

The corpse seemed so real that Lyons wondered if somehow he crossed into another dimension. Blood stained a wall above the motionless form. A flight of stairs ascended to the next floor. The rungs appeared to be too even and showed no sign of wear, yet otherwise seemed real enough. Lyons was amazed when he began to mount the stairs. His legs rose and descended on the risers. The sensation of actually climbing the stairs seemed genuine. He knew that wasn't really possible, but it all seemed very real. Lyons wondered if he would feel pain if an opponent managed to nail him with a bullet.

He reached the next floor, stepping into a corridor with a long, dark red carpet and subdued light from ceiling bulbs. A figure moved by a doorway, and Lyons saw a weapon in his opponent's fist. He knelt low and pointed his pistol. A face that appeared to belong to a male Caucasian, roughly forty years old, turned to stare at Lyons. The Able Team leader fired and his third opponent collapsed to the floor.

Suddenly, another shape charged from a different doorway. Lyons saw the blur of a dark-clad enemy and a boxlike weapon pointed at him. It appeared to be an Ingram MAC-10. Lyons realized the machine pistol had poor accuracy and a limited range, yet it fired 9 mm rounds close to a thousand a minute. The distance involved eliminated the weapon's flaws.

Lyons rolled for cover by the edge of the stairwell, feeling his body tumble over the lip and into the risers. Images whirled as he hit the stairs and felt the painful hammering along his limbs and torso.

The big ex-cop heard the metallic snarl of a full-auto weapon above. He sprawled across a landing and glanced up the stairs. Those stairs damn sure felt real when he took his tumble.

The commando had managed to hold on to the pistol. He thrust his arm high as the gun-wielding figure appeared at the head of the stairs. Lyons squeezed two shots, his arm jerking with the Magnum recoil. His opponent jackknifed and plunged headfirst down the stairs. Lyons rose and moved aside to clear the path for his fallen enemy. The MAC-10 clattered on the stairs near the vanquished foe.

Lyons figured he might need more firepower. With the pistol in one hand, he reached with the other for the Ingram. His fingers passed through the weapon and clutched only air. He drew back, startled once more. Of course, he couldn't pick it up. It wasn't real. None of this was real, but the illusion proved so convincing Lyons had forgotten. The pistol in his hand wasn't really a .357 Colt Python with a 6-round capacity. It was a training device that operated in the computerized virtual reality realm and didn't need to be reloaded during the "game."

He prepared to mount the stairs once more. The steps vanished beneath his feet. Walls dissolved, and the bodies of his terrorist opponents disappeared. Lyons stared at his own feet and legs, clad in orange fabric streaked by a network of blue cords. Blue screen surrounded the Able Team leader. He was aware he lay on his back, a harness belt around his waist. Lyons wore an orange coverall suit and gloves. The pistol in his fist no longer appeared to be a Colt Python revolver. It was a bulky plastic gizmo with a solid barrel that could launch no projectile.

"Congratulations, Mr. Carlson," a voice said from a wall insert. "The exercise is over. You won."

"I did?" Lyons replied with surprise.

"You killed all the bad guys," the voice confirmed. "That means you won. We'll help you get out of that gear."

He heard a door open and footfalls approach. Lyons tried to crane his neck to see, but the helmet limited movement. Hands soon pulled the headgear free. Lyons stared at the wide amber lens and the plastic shell he had formerly worn during the exercise.

The moon face of Robert Yong smiled at Lyons. His thick glasses exaggerated the Asian cast of his hazel eyes. The director of operations for Kumo Shima Enterprises, U.S. Division, tucked the helmet under his arm while an assistant helped Lyons out of the harness.

"How did you like it, Mr. Carlson?" Yong asked.

"I'm not sure if I liked it, exactly," the Able Team commando answered as he took a deep breath. "It's definitely realistic. Before you plan to market something like this as a computer game to the general public, you'd better make sure players sign an agreement that they accept responsibility for any physical or emotional trauma they may experience."

Yong uttered a short laugh. "We won't be marketing this to the general public. This is strictly for training personnel like yourself. Police, government agents, security personnel and the military will be our clients for this program. We believe it is the best simulation of actual combat available today."

"I wouldn't argue that," Lyons admitted as he sat up on the cot. "I thought I was going to break a rib on those stairs. I didn't expect the images to seem that real."

"That sensation was caused by a network of tubes in the suit," Yong explained. "They expanded when signaled by the events taking place during the exercise to simulate a sensation of the stairs as you fell. A CO_2 jet is used to jam the expanded tubes inward, causing the jarring sensation and adding to the realism. But I assure you there was never any risk you might actually suffer any injury aside from a slight bruise that will go away in a few minutes."

"Incredible," Lyons said. "Is that what caused the sensation of walking on a hard surface when my feet were really in the air?"

"Correct," Yong confirmed. "Pressure is put into the soles of your feet through the boots. It varies depending on the type of surface a subject steps on during the program and how much force is exerted by the person. If you walk on a grassy surface, the sensation is quite different than you would feel if you kicked in a door during the exercise."

"What if I had been shot?"

"You would feel a sharp jab at the point of projectile impact registered by the mainframe," Yong explained. "The computer would evaluate the most likely result of the wound. If it determined the wound would immobilize a limb, say an arm, the tubes would expand and compress your arm at the joints to render it useless. A mortal wound would immediately terminate the exercise and declare the terrorists as the winners."

"I've got to admit I'm impressed."

"State-of-the-art computer-generated images with laser projection on an advanced 3-D screen are set inside the helmet. The scenes play out all around your head, producing a full effect, along with the sensations produced by the suit, gloves and boots...not to mention the training pistol."

"Yeah," Lyons said. "Seemed to kick just like a real .357 Magnum."

"That's what it was programmed for in your case because that was the weapon you said you favored," Yong stated. "It can just as easily be adjusted to reproduce the recoil of a 9 mm Parabellum round, a .45, .38 Special, .44 Magnum or a 10 mm. We don't reproduce any smaller caliber recoils because they wouldn't be serious combat weapons. Maybe a civilian model will include .22 recoil for people who want to practice target shooting."

"Well, I can sure see why Kumo Shima has been so successful," Lyons said. "I've done this virtual reality stuff before, and this is a hell of a lot more realistic than anything I've used or even heard of."

"So real you even tried to grab that gun the terrorist dropped on the stairs," Yong commented.

"You knew about that?" Lyons asked with raised eyebrows.

"Of course," the director replied. "We tracked your progress on a monitor. The scenes you saw were produced by our mainframe and recorded on video. You're welcome to see it. We usually show the tapes so mistakes can be pointed out to subjects, but you didn't make any serious mistakes. Not many men can survive a gunfight against four-to-one odds. They must train you very well for that elite section of the FBI. That is who you work for, correct?"

"That's my ID. I thought it was understood that my

work is undercover and I can't have my face showing up on videotape.''

"No one will recognize you on the tape," Yong assured him. "The image projected into the system is taken of you while you're wearing the suit and helmet. Your real movements in this room were transmitted into the mainframe and altered slightly to act more naturally in the virtual reality setting. You should be pleased by the performance. A couple hesitations may be noted, but that was certainly because you weren't prepared for the experience to be as real as you discovered it to be.''

"Okay," Lyons said with a grin. "I like that reason.''

"It will be interesting to see how well your two friends score. They probably won't score as high. No one else has since we started this program. You must have seen some real combat to have such extraordinary reflexes.''

Lyons didn't respond.

"I only ask to get a better idea if our system is similar to the real battlefield conditions you've experienced.''

"It comes pretty close," Lyons assured him. "So what's next?''

"Get some rest," Yong replied. "You've earned it. We have a limited number of chambers, and we have to use this one for another subject. Tomorrow, we'll have another program set for you. Something more difficult to put your skills to a greater test. We'll see if you break any more records.''

"That should be interesting," Lyons replied with a nod.

"I assure you it will be.''

4

The Bell helicopter cruised above the treetops of the Shenandoah National Park. Snow settled along pine needles of the branches, but the sky was clear. The accumulation was far less than what Bolan had encountered in Alaska, and weather reports predicted no more snow would fall that year in the Virginia region.

The mountain range was beautiful during the first days of spring. Mack Bolan seldom had an opportunity to enjoy the natural splendor. New leaves had already sprouted on many trees and bushes. Deer roamed the forests, and Bolan even spotted a black bear near a stream, no doubt recently aroused from hibernation. It was a sure sign winter had ended and warmer days were on their way.

Jack Grimaldi piloted the chopper with the ease of a professional who had made the trip countless times before, barely glancing at his instruments. They approached the Blue Ridge Mountains and soon saw the rock wall of one of the largest and tallest features of the range. The craggy profile could have been that of an ancient Titan, turned to stone and punished for the rebellion against the gods. This was Stony Man Mountain. For the Executioner and Grimaldi, it meant they were almost home.

Stony Man Farm wasn't exactly Bolan's home. He

hadn't had a permanent residence for many years. A home didn't really suit his life-style. However, the Farm was his base of operations and populated by his most trusted friends and allies.

The Farm wouldn't have attracted much attention to a pilot or passenger unaware of its true function. It appeared to be a working farm, and part of the land did grow and harvest crops, although the fields were unattended this day. Aside from a rather isolated position, the farm didn't seem unusual. The two-story main house was larger than one might expect but not enough to impress a casual observer. A tabloid reporter had heard about the remote farm with a big house and a helicopter pad, and launched a brief investigation, yet soon lost interest when the property didn't turn out to be registered in the name of an eccentric celebrity.

Grimaldi flew to the north flank and hovered over the landing field. The chopper descended as two Jeeps approached to meet them. Bolan recognized Hal Brognola and Barbara Price in one vehicle. John "Cowboy" Kissinger drove the other. The Bell copter touched down, and the Executioner pushed open the door to emerge. He ducked his head slightly as the big rotor blades continued to whirl, walking to the Jeep with Brognola in the back seat and Price at the wheel.

"Doesn't seem like spring yet," Brognola remarked. "But I bet it's still warmer than Alaska this time of year."

"You'd win that bet," Bolan replied.

He slid into the front seat beside Price. The lovely blond lady greeted him with a wide smile. A bulky jacket concealed her excellent curves, but Bolan knew what was hidden from view. He swung his duffel bag of gear into the back seat and allowed Brognola to find an empty place for it.

The Jeep headed for the main house. Grimaldi would follow after he finished a general inspection of the helicopter. Brognola rummaged inside his winter coat to find a cigar, chomping on the unlit cigar before he spoke.

"Cops in Alaska are puzzled by your sudden disappearance," he began, "but they've got enough on DiCarlo and his boys to put them away for the rest of their lives. DiCarlo was sort of unfinished business for you."

"A medium-size fish that got away during a campaign against the Mob in Jersey some time ago," Bolan answered. "Pete DiCarlo was a minor capo, but he could have become more if his phony terrorist blackmail scheme had worked. He was never smart enough to be a big player, and somebody would've nailed him sooner or later. I just got him before he could do any more damage."

"Nice work," the big Fed remarked. "As usual. You didn't mention that Sutton got wasted at the Watley Petroleum base. Didn't you arrive right after it happened?"

"Everything was over by the time I arrived," the Executioner replied. "Sutton, one of his bodyguards and Paul Greely were already bagged and ready for a medical examiner. I didn't mention it because it had nothing to do with my mission. Greely killed Sutton in front of enough witnesses to confirm he acted alone. Strange incident, but it wasn't connected with the terrorists."

"Wasn't Greely the chief of security at the oil base?" Price asked. "Pretty weird that he'd snap and kill the vice president of the company for no apparent reason.''

"Well," Brognola began, "I've heard about people going crazy in the arctic. Even well-trained professionals have been known to flip out in that sort of isolated environment."

"Maybe," Bolan said, "but the Watley outpost wasn't exactly an igloo. I met Greely, and he didn't seem to be unbalanced or on the edge to me. He was obviously dealing with a lot of stress, but that seemed normal when the terrorists were hitting the pipelines."

"I guess you hear people say all the time that some guy was a nice fellow and never seemed weird until he climbed a tower or headed for a fast-food joint to kill two dozen people," Brognola commented. "If we knew what makes some men go nuts, we could stop them before it happened."

They reached the house. The trio left the Jeep, and Price punched in the access code to the front door. It appeared to be wood, but the door was steel and sturdy enough to hold up under most cannon fire. They entered the hall to discover Aaron Kurtzman emerging from the computer center. The wheelchair-bound expert in artificial intelligence and cybernetics seldom ventured beyond his high-tech lair. Nicknamed The Bear before an enemy bullet sentenced him to spend the rest of his life in the chair, Kurtzman remained a burly, sometimes gruff character. He was also a genius, and no one at Stony Man could imagine anyone better suited to handle the computer system that was so vital to their organization.

"What happened, Aaron?" Brognola began as he approached. "You run out of coffee? That is what you call that awful black stuff you drink all day?"

Kurtzman grunted as he rolled his chair forward. He steadfastly refused to acquire a motorized chair, and his thickly muscled arms testified to his enormous upper body strength.

"Every so often even I need to get away from the computer screens," he declared. "Especially when the world seems to be even more nuts than usual. Well, at least according to the data coming in. By the way, Striker...hello."

"Hello, Bear," Bolan replied with a grin.

"We were just talking about how people go crazy for no apparent reason," Brognola stated. "Of course, you know what happened up at the oil outpost in Alaska?"

"Yeah," Kurtzman confirmed. "That sort of thing seems to happen more often."

"And no one can predict who will crack under the strain," Price added. "Remember how shocked everyone was when Vince Foster committed suicide? A couple years later, Admiral Boorda, chief of U.S. naval operations, killed himself...apparently because he was upset about a magazine article that questioned his right to wear a Vietnam combat decoration."

"Yeah," Kurtzman began. "That happens, Barb. Still, two high-level captains of industry getting killed by their own security personnel in less than twenty-four hours is pretty unusual."

"Another hotshot executive type bought it the same as Sutton?" Brognola asked with surprise.

Kurtzman nodded and said, "Almost identical situation. A guy named Brittly was head of Chapman Robotics—third or fourth biggest U.S. manufacturer of industrial robots. Sort of things they use on assembly lines these days and a few more sophisticated projects for the military like mechanical mine detectors and probe devices. Anyway, Brittly was killed by his top security expert. Supposedly, the guy went to Brittly's office for a standard report about factory security at the main branch. Nobody expected anything like this to happen, but the son of a bitch just opened fire and killed Brittly as he sat behind his desk.''

"Jesus," Brognola rasped. "Is he under arrest?"

"They didn't get the chance. The security guard killed himself. Blew his brains out shortly after he took out Brittly. I don't remember his name, but I can find it easy enough. Hell, the story is probably on the TV news by now. I can access his personal files if you want to know more about him."

"We have enough work to deal with. It's not our job, and there isn't much we can do now anyway."

"Guess you're right, Hal," Kurtzman said with a shrug. "Well, DiCarlo is sure washed up in Alaska. Cops and Feds took what you handed them to round up the rest of his gang, Striker."

"That's how I like a mission to end," Bolan replied. "I wouldn't mind using a room here to catch up on some sleep."

"Sure," Brognola assured him. "You've earned it."

Jack Grimaldi and John Kissinger entered the building. The weapons smith marched forward and offered a muscled hand to Bolan. The two men shook hands.

"Good to have you back, Striker," he declared. "If you don't have another project lined up, I know something you may want to try."

"Not again," Kurtzman groaned and rolled his eyes toward the ceiling. "He just got back from a mission, John. Give him a break."

"I didn't mean he had to leave right this minute,"

Kissinger insisted. "Hell, he'd have to get on the Kumo Shima waiting list anyway. They're getting a lot of business, and they'll get a lot more when word gets out how good their program is."

"Kumo Shima?" Bolan asked with a raised eyebrow.

"Japanese for 'Cloud Island' or something like that," Brognola explained. "It's a computer company that's just gone international and specializes in virtual reality stuff. Claims to be the most advanced on the market today."

"I'll back up that claim," Kissinger declared. "I heard they planned a demonstration at a show in L.A. three days ago, and I flew out to attend. Tried out their VR combat-training program designed for cops and Feds and so forth. I was really stunned by how real it seemed. The images moved like real people, not like typical animation. Weapons looked and sounded genuine. The pistol in my hand recoiled in a realistic manner."

"And we've been hearing about it ever since," Kurtzman said with a sigh.

"You're just jealous because the Kumo Shima system can produce better virtual reality images than even your computer mainframe," Kissinger stated. "When Able Team returns, the guys will tell you the same."

Able Team consisted of three veteran warriors and longtime friends of the Executioner. Carl Lyons commanded the team. He had earned his nickname "Ironman" due to his exceptional physical strength and determination. Rosario Blancanales and Hermann Schwarz had served with Mack Bolan in the Army and on numerous campaigns against the Mob before the creation of Stony Man.

"The Cowboy was so impressed by this Kumo Shima VR program he thinks all our combat personnel can benefit from it," Brognola explained. "The only major domestic terrorist activity we had to deal with was being handled by you in Alaska, Striker. So, it seemed to be a good time for Able Team to try this fancy VR training program."

"Of course," Kissinger began, "they'll have a more detailed experience than I had with the demonstration in L.A. I'm also curious to see how well our guys score compared to the others taking the course. A number of Feds, police officers and security personnel are there. Bet Able Team puts them all to shame."

"I didn't know we were in competition with them," Bolan remarked. "Personally, I've had enough real combat recently. I don't want to spend any time with virtual reality versions."

"Maybe you'll be more interested after Able Team returns from Texas," Kissinger suggested.

"They have an L.A. in Texas?" Grimaldi asked.

"The demo was in Los Angeles," Kissinger explained, "but Kumo Shima's U.S. base is in Texas, outside Dallas."

"Why don't we discuss this later?" Price suggested. "Striker needs to get some rest."

Bolan followed Price out of the room. The others discreetly looked away as they departed.

AMERICAN TELEVISION was strange, Major Choi Sung thought as he stared at the small screen in the hotel room. He found the advertising obnoxious and tasteless, blatant efforts to appeal to the greed and selfishness that corrupted the capitalist masses. Commercials peddled expensive luxury items as if the merchandise held the key to happiness and total satisfaction.

Democracy, Choi thought with disgust. It preached freedom and equality, but the reality was quite different. The United States of America was supposed to be the great shining example of democracy. Yet, he had seen the gulf between classes in America. The rich and the upper middle class enjoyed wealth and security while the poor could only suffer and try to survive in a society that gave lip service to its plight, but cut funds for needed services.

The Americans criticized communism and the repressive government of North Korea. Choi found that offensive. Perhaps communism also exaggerated claims of equality for the masses. Choi certainly enjoyed a privileged position in his homeland as a field-grade officer and high-ranking member of the Party, but he believed he had earned that right. North Korea maintained law and order. His country didn't tolerate dissidents or protesters, let alone the street gangs and gangsters that seemed to roam the streets of America without fear of the authorities.

His contempt for democracy in general and the United States in particular increased the more time he spent in America. The capitalists' most popular medium—television—contributed to his attitude. Mindless entertainment was presented to the public via TV. Violence, adultery, premarital sex and an attitude of disrespect toward almost everything filled these broadcasts. The commercials seemed most vile to Choi. Sex was used to sell everything from automobiles to deodorant.

Yet, he was strangely fascinated by what he saw on the TV screen. He felt compelled to learn how self-indulgent the medium could be. If he found the material appealing or entertaining, Choi wouldn't have admitted this even to himself.

Another offensive commercial ended and a program began. Choi realized this was a rerun of an old show because it was in black-and-white. The lyrics of a song with a sailor-style tune intrigued Choi as he watched a boat depart a harbor. A knock at the door disturbed his concentration. Choi reached for a shoe box containing his Browning pistol as he rose from the chair. He carried the box to the door.

"Who is it?"

"Robert Yong," a voice replied.

Choi set aside the box and unlocked the door. Yong entered the room. He gazed up at the major through the thick lenses of his glasses. Choi disliked everything about Yong, including his appearance. Yong looked like a bookworm. He was overweight, soft and pale. He reminded Choi of a fat maggot with a high IQ.

"*Choi ssi anyong hasipnika*," Yong began.

"Speak English," the major insisted. "I need to practice the language as much as possible and your grasp of Korean is very poor."

"I'm sorry," Yong replied. "My parents didn't speak much of their native language at home. They wanted their children to be as American as possible. They didn't realize that regardless of how well an Asian-American speaks English, dresses, behaves and tries to think as an American, white America will always consider him to be Asian and treat him as an unwanted foreigner."

"That doesn't surprise me," Choi commented as he locked the door. "I've noticed the so-called melting pot in this country is mostly white on top. The majority of faces on this television have certainly been white, and the concepts presented are from a Western capitalist point of view.''

"Well," Yong began as he glanced at the black-and-white images on the screen, "that show was made in the sixties. They have more Asians, blacks and Latinos on TV now. Mostly tokens, of course, but they try to convince us they're more open-minded now.''

"Perhaps," Choi said, "but this old program is the only thing I've seen so far on your American television that seems to have any substance.''

Yong was startled by this remark. The rerun on the TV was from a program series Yong had always considered to be among the most idiotic in the history of any media.

"I was surprised by this myself," Choi continued. "The story line was explained in a type of ballad. A small cruise boat is lost at sea and eventually wrecks on the shore of an unknown island. The hero appears to be a common sailor, yet acknowledged for his courage and skill. The actor who plays the part is rather common-looking, painfully thin and doesn't fit the role of the usual Western idea of a heroic character. That makes him all the more representative of the working-class masses.''

"It's *Gilligan's Island*," Yong stated.

"So you've seen it?" Choi asked with interest. "You know that it features characters of different social status, economic and education levels. Among the passengers are a millionaire capitalist, his spoiled rich wife, a female movie star and a scientist.''

"Don't forget Mary Ann," Yong said dryly. "I hate to disappoint you, Major, but this show isn't about the class struggle carried out in an isolated area without a government to favor the privileged elite. It's just a sitcom."

"Sitcom?" Choi asked, unfamiliar with the term. "They tried to suggest a sense of irony and tragedy about this situation because the cruise was only supposed to last three hours."

"More like four or five years followed by an eternity in syndication," Yong said with a sigh. "If you want to watch something intelligent on television, you might try CNN, PBS, the Discovery Channel or Arts & Entertainment."

"I've probably wasted too much time watching this nonsense, but I thought it might help me grasp certain American slang expressions."

Choi turned off the TV. He seemed annoyed, and Yong wondered if the major was embarrassed because he had thought *Gilligan's Island* to be a great drama with social and political commentary.

The Korean could be a scary guy when he was angry. Choi stood about six feet tall and still appeared to be pretty fit for a man pushing fifty, Yong observed. His hair was clipped so short he appeared bald at first glance, and that seemed to match his hard features and generally unpleasant nature.

Choi was meaner than he looked. The major had killed a lot of people and probably ordered the executions for hundreds of others. Yong realized Choi didn't care for his company, and the feeling was certainly mutual. But, then, they hadn't been brought together to become friends.

"I've got some new recruits for our VR combat program, Major. Several are promising. Three in particular stand out for their skill, reflexes and physical ability. They claim to be part of a special section of the FBI, but they're more than that. I hacked into the FBI personnel mainframe to check out their claims. The computer has them on file, but details are classified with a security code. The restricted access is so tight even the director couldn't break into it. Their authority level is incredible. It goes all the way to the White House.''

"The White House?" Choi asked with surprise. "You think they might be some elite enforcement or security arm for the President?"

"It's possible," Yong answered. "They're certainly the most impressive subjects we've had at the VR center. They scored high on every level. Exceptionally intelligent, extremely skilled and potentially deadly. We pitched them against four-to-one odds, and they took out multiple opponents in gun battles as if they've done it a hundred times before."

"Maybe they have," Choi commented. "Are they getting special treatment?"

"Not yet," Yong said. "I wanted to check with you first and maybe contact Kykosawa. If they are directly linked to the White House, this could be too big a step to take without agreement by Kykosawa, as well as yourself."

"He's in Japan, and it will take too long to contact him and wait for him to evaluate the situation. We need to start work on these three superagents as soon as possible. Such an opportunity must not slip from our grasp, Yong."

"Okay," Yong said with a sigh. "We go for it."

"Right," Choi confirmed, smiling as he nodded his head. "We go for it."

5

The plane would leave in less than an hour, Robert Pliny thought. He checked his watch for the fifth time in as many minutes since he stood at the head of the marble steps of the Capitol Building. Five minutes wasn't a long time unless one was eager to be somewhere else.

Pliny might have been less anxious if he had encountered newspaper and television reporters. Perhaps the cold, damp weather discouraged the press. More likely they simply didn't care why Pliny waited in front of the most famous federal legislative building in the United States. The junior congressman hadn't held office long enough to attract much interest from the media. Pliny was neither a firebrand speaker on the floor of the House of Representatives nor a target of an investigation of a major scandal.

A drab star in the political firmament wasn't deemed worthy of attention by the press. Pliny hadn't earned any interest as champion of a cause. He also realized his election had gained little national attention. Pliny was chosen because his predecessor was unpopular with the voters in his state. They hadn't really voted for him as much as voted against the other guy.

Yet, Pliny wanted the fame and recognition as an honored member of the U.S. congress. He hoped to achieve a new image as an important, active member of an economic-and-trade committee. His trip to Europe was the first step in that direction.

To accomplish that, he needed to get to the airport and his limo was late. This delay couldn't be avoided because the driver had to pick up Jim Sell and Claude Johnson for the trip. Pliny considered himself lucky to get two bodyguards with such professional backgrounds and experience. Maybe the cold war was over, but enough anti-American attitudes and terrorism continued in Europe to convince Pliny he needed good security.

Johnson and Sell were pros and constantly worked on improving their skills. They had prepared for the trip by taking an advanced defensive driving course that included escape and evasion in streets where one drove on the left-hand side of the road. They took crash language studies in French, German and Italian so they would have some working vocabularies in an emergency. The pair had just returned from an advanced program supposed to help hone their combat skills as well. Good men, Pliny thought, but he didn't want to miss his flight because they were late.

"Bob?" a voice spoke from the entrance of the building. "I thought that was you. What's the matter?"

Pliny turned to face Andrew Maxwell. The stocky, gray-haired senior congressman was a well-known member of congress and belonged to the same party as Pliny. Maxwell was the sort of friend Pliny tried to cultivate since he came to Washington. He wanted to impress the veteran congressman as being more than an unabashed sycophant, although he had already kissed Maxwell's ass enough for the senior man to remember him.

"Hello, Congressman," Pliny greeted. "Nothing's wrong. I'm just waiting for my limo."

"Limo?" Maxwell asked with a raised eyebrow. "Thought you young fellows tried to avoid those ostentatious displays of privilege because the public thinks we get too many benefits already."

"This is for a trade and economic evaluation for my committee," Pliny explained. He tried to sound casual as he watched Maxwell for any sign of approval. "I have to visit three European trade partners, attend a couple summits. That sort of thing."

"Congratulations," Maxwell said. "Will you be gone long?"

"Two weeks."

"What countries?"

"Italy, France and Germany. Probably England as well."

"Germany was more fun when it was divided," the senior congressman remarked. "I could have recommended some great spots in West Germany. I can't say if they're the same now. The French can be sort of snotty, but if you tip them enough they're okay. I like Italy better, only watch your ass over there. A lot of pickpockets and petty thieves are running around Rome."

"I'm more worried about terrorists."

"That threat is exaggerated," Maxwell assured him. "More likely somebody will try to grab your camera than hold you ransom. You have a pen or minirecorder? I can give you the names of some good restaurants in Rome and Paris."

"Great," Pliny replied eagerly.

He was searching his pockets for a pen and notepad as a long black vehicle rolled up to the curb. Damn,

Pliny thought with frustration. The limo would have to arrive just as he was trying to score points with Maxwell. He started to explain the situation to the senior legislator as he descended the steps. Maxwell followed and insisted Pliny jot down at least two French restaurants.

The side doors to the limousine opened. Jim Sell stepped out from one side, his tall, lean frame and close-cropped blond hair making him easy to identify from a distance. Claude Johnson emerged from the opposite side of the vehicle. Shorter than Sell, Johnson was the more muscular of the pair. The African-American bodyguard also took more care with his appearance and wardrobe than Sell. Johnson's tailored suits with matching neckties made him look more like a male model. Sell's clothes always seemed too large and baggy. He probably figured that style helped him conceal his holstered weapon and allowed greater freedom of movement.

"I take it they already made hotel reservations for you," Maxwell commented. "In the future, check with me. I know the best."

"Thank you," Pliny assured him as he waved at Johnson and Sell. "I'm coming—"

The bodyguards suddenly reached inside their jackets and drew pistols. Pliny gasped in astonishment and fear. He glanced about for whatever threat had triggered the response. Two shots roared in unison, the reports tumbling together to become a single exaggerated noise. Pain ripped into Pliny's torso at the same instant. His nerves screamed with agony so intense he didn't feel the marble when he slammed into the steps. The back of his skull connected with a stone riser and mercifully rendered him unconscious while his life oozed from the bullet holes.

"My God!" Maxwell exclaimed as he raised his briefcase in a reflex reaction.

Sell and Johnson triggered their SIG-Sauer pistols again. A 9 mm slug punched through the valise shield and whatever Maxwell carried in the case. The projectile met more resistance from a winter coat and scarf. Maxwell felt as if a sledgehammer struck his chest. He began to fall as another bullet drilled his soft belly above the navel.

The limo driver shifted gears and stomped the gas pedal. But in his panic, he had put the car in reverse. It bolted backward, hopped the curb and skidded along the sidewalk. Sell swung his pistol toward the vehicle, eyes open wide, face contorted with an expression that resembled a trapped and dangerous animal.

The bodyguard squeezed off two shots. Both 9 mm rounds struck the windshield, creating a spiderweb pattern as it cracked the sturdy glass. The second bullet smashed through the weakened barrier, catching the driver in the face. Blood poured down the man's cheek as he slumped from view.

Two uniformed figures, bundled in winter jackets and fur-lined caps, jogged toward the scene. One cop fumbled with his holstered weapon, unaccustomed to the chore and more clumsy due to his gloves and thick clothing. The other officer managed to draw his side arm, but Johnson shot him twice in the chest before the cop could try to take aim.

The other policeman saw his partner fall and dived to the pavement, still unable to clear his gun from leather. Johnson tracked the movement and fired into the prone figure. A bullet sliced into the cop's cap, burrowing a lethal tunnel into his skull.

"Help me!" Maxwell cried as loud as the hot pain in his intestines allowed. "Please…"

The scream drew Sell's attention. The blond gunman stepped closer and fired twice to silence the senior congressman. Pliny didn't stir and appeared to be dead already, but Sell cursed and pumped another 9 mm round into the side of his boss's head. Brains and skull debris splashed across the steps of the Capitol.

More uniformed shapes appeared at the head of the stairs. The security personnel assigned to the building were more accustomed to public relations than combat. The revolver in one officer's hands trembled as he tried to take aim. Sell spotted him and raised his SIG-Sauer. Both men opened fire. The guard's .38 round ricocheted off marble half a yard from Sell's left foot. The frenzied gunman scored another deadly hit. The patrolman cried out, clutching his bullet-punctured stomach. He stumbled forward, lost his balance and plunged headfirst down the stairs.

The second security officer had sought cover behind a marble pillar. He heard the screams and groans of his comrade. The sounds grew more faint as the man's body slammed down the steps. Finally, the guard couldn't utter more than a weak moan as he completed the bone-breaking tumble.

Sirens sounded. Police response wasn't usually remarkable in D.C., but cops paid more attention to the federal buildings, especially since terrorists had targeted such sights in the past. Johnson and Sell saw the flashing lights in the street. Traffic parted along Independence and Constitution avenues as the cops approached.

The berserk bodyguards headed for the limo that had rolled to a stop, rear end jamming into the nose of a smaller vehicle. Johnson opened the driver's door and dragged out the stunned, wounded chauffeur. He dumped the man on the pavement and calmly shot him in the back of the head.

Sell and Johnson climbed into the limo as the police cars advanced. The vehicle bolted forward with Johnson at the wheel. Cop cars screeched their brakes as they abruptly stopped in the path of the limo. Johnson and Sell seemed unconcerned and drove into the nearest vehicle. Metal crunched on metal.

The impact crumpled the police-car door. The hood to the limo popped open as steam and hot fluid spewed from the ruptured radiator. The bodyguards emerged from the limo, pistols spitting fire. Uniformed figures also appeared from other vehicles with weapons drawn. One cop stopped a 9 mm round with his forehead the moment he stepped from his car. Another was hit in the center of his chest.

Stunned by the crash, the officer of the smashed car still sat behind the wheel. Johnson pumped a round through the side window, blasting the helpless victim. Brains and blood sprayed across the dashboard.

Gunfire erupted from both sides, but the bodyguards ducked behind the open limo doors. Bullets hammered the heavy steel. Sell swung around the edge of a door, his clothes stained and torn by blood and bullets. Despite the wounds he suffered, Sell fired his SIG-Sauer at the cops until he exhausted the last round and his weapon clicked on empty.

Two shotguns bellowed from the police car. The officers with riot weapons nailed Sell with a double dose of 12-gauge pellets. Buckshot nearly ripped the man in two. What remained of his pulped, bloodied form sank to the pavement.

Johnson never even noticed that his partner went down. The remaining gunman fired over the door top he used for a shield. Another shotgun blast responded. Johnson jerked back as the SIG-Sauer hurled from his grasp. Blood spurted from the middle knuckle of his trigger finger. The rest had been amputated by the buckshot.

"Fuck you goddamn Klanners!" he exclaimed.

Johnson yanked up a pant leg and drew a compact .380 pistol from an ankle holster. He held it in his uninjured fist, thumbed the safety and waited for a lull in the fire. A cop even shouted for the others to hold their fire, probably aware the SIG-Sauer had been shot from Johnson's hand and unaware he had a backup piece.

A shot snarled from a direction Johnson hadn't expected. He had forgotten about the security guard behind the marble pillar at the top of the Capitol Building stairs. The guard had waited for an opportunity to use his weapon and saw Johnson busy with the cops. He had a clear target from his elevated position. The guard fired at the man by the limo. Claude Johnson twitched as two or more .38 rounds struck his lower back. Johnson stumbled from the shelter of the car door. A salvo of police bullets slammed into the wounded bodyguard, sending his ravaged body across the pavement.

"Somebody call an ambulance!" a voice ordered. "Tell them to send as many as they can as fast as possible! Tell them we've got officers down as well as civilians!"

"Ambulances are already on the way," someone replied.

Three cops slowly approached the corpse of Sell

while another trio checked Johnson. There was no doubt the mangled bodies were dead, but the cops didn't intend to take any chances and kept their weapons trained on the pair.

"What the hell got into these bastards?" an officer asked, aware no one could really answer the question.

No one tried.

6

Hal Brognola looked at the face of the President on the wall screen in the Stony Man War Room. The real-time broadcast was a computer transmission from the White House. The special high-tech communications was part of a secure satellite link used exclusively by Stony Man.

The President appeared haggard and worried. Brognola had expected that. His organization existed to deal with problems, and the Man in the Oval Office didn't call seeking support on issues or asking for campaign funds. The President contacted Stony Man only when he didn't know who else could deal with such a crisis.

"I expected you to get in touch, sir," Brognola stated. "Two congressmen are dead. Four D.C. cops, a security patrolman and the limo driver were also killed when Congressman Pliny's bodyguards went berserk. A couple of the police in the hospital look like they won't survive the next twenty-four hours. If you include Sell and Johnson, that will bring the body count to an even dozen if those cops don't make it."

"So you are familiar with this incident?"

"Can't say that exactly, because it just happened," the big Fed replied. "But we know about it. Data rolled into our computers minutes after it occurred. We probably knew about it before you did. The system immediately evaluated it as top-level urgency and shot it straight to the Bear's den with an emergency-code alarm.''

''Bear's den?'' the President asked with a frown.

''You know Aaron. We call him the Bear.''

''Oh, yes. You don't really seem too surprised by this carnage.''

''Trust me, I was surprised, but Aaron wasn't. He figured there was a connection to a couple other violent incidents over the past forty-eight hours. Two top business executives were also murdered by their security personnel, who apparently went insane for no reason.''

''Do these killers have anything in common?'' the President asked.

''So far the only thing that seems to connect them is they all seemed very professional and reliable,'' Brognola answered ''I've seen the files on those guys. They were well trained, with a fair amount of experience. One guy had been involved with law enforcement for two decades and another used to be with the Secret Service.''

''Oh, that's encouraging,'' the President said dryly.

''Obviously, Sell and Johnson were pretty good with a gun or they wouldn't have claimed so many victims. Unfortunately, their pistols were loaded with special NATO 9 mm ammo, armor-piercing rounds not available to the general public or even most police. They had permits from the federal government for the ammo because they were assigned to protect a U.S. congressman. The D.C. cops wore vests, but that didn't help much.''

''This sounds worse with each sentence you utter.''

''No one had any reason to be suspicious of these guys. According to their files, they were like a couple of Boy Scouts. They appear to have done well in school. No radical politics, history of drug use or mental disorders. Johnson was decorated twice for valor when he was with the St. Louis Police Department and again when he worked for DEA. It seems he switched over to guarding legislators because he figured it was less risky and he didn't want his wife and kids to worry about him.''

"So they were wonderful fellows who just snapped?" the President asked and shook his head. "There has to be a reason, Hal."

"I agree, but we don't know what it is yet. Johnson and Sell worked together, but there is no evidence they knew the other two. They varied in age, religious background, political affiliation and membership in organizations.''

"Too bad the police didn't manage to take one of them alive.''

"If Sell or Johnson hadn't been killed, they might have taken their own lives. The other two did.''

"Suicidal as well as homicidal,'' the President said with a sigh. "I want Stony Man on this, Hal. Apparently, you already are.''

"I dispatched one of my people to the scene, and we're working on it from this end with data from the computers. I can't send out an action team until we know where the enemy is. If there is an enemy.''

"You think these people are just going insane?''

"I think there's a connection,'' the big Fed replied. "But a number of postal workers have gone on the rampage, gunning down fellow workers. I don't think there has been any evidence of a conspiracy involved in those incidents.''

"People have gone berserk at other places—business, restaurants and colleges. Even playgrounds filled with schoolchildren. My administration has supported national gun control laws to try to restrict the sale of assault rifles to the public and enforced a waiting period for handguns. Perhaps we need more restrictions.''

"Well," Brognola began, "laws and policies are your business. We don't make those decisions at Stony Man. Still, I don't think you're going to stop lunatics going on murder sprees by more gun-control laws.''

"So how do you suggest we stop people from going crazy and killing innocent people?'' the President asked.

"There's more than one reason why that sort of thing happens. In most cases, the person who does it is usually a stressed-out, broken loser who thinks his world has come to an end so he might as well take a few people with him. Probably happens more often because the world has become a more stressful and confusing place. Things are changing too fast. No one feels secure in their jobs, on the streets, in their homes. They figure they can wind up out of work, killed on their way home by some crazy street gang and they're afraid their homes are unsafe due to radon, asbestos and fallout from nearby nuclear power plants.''

"Those fears are probably out of proportion with reality,'' the President stated. "But we're trying to deal with those problems.''

"Maybe," Brognola said, "but I don't have to tell you the public doesn't have a hell of a lot of faith in the government.''

"Don't forget you and your outfit are part of that government or at least attached to it.''

"Yeah," the big Fed admitted, "but we've never added to any problems. Stony Man is one of the least expensive organizations associated with the government, and none can match our success record. That's why you want us to look into this business with the kill-crazy bodyguards.''

"I don't want you to look into it," the Man replied. "I want you to solve it and add that to your list of successful missions."

"We're on it, Mr. President. Who else do you have on this? It's best if we don't cross paths if we don't have to. Sometimes investigating federal agents can be more an obstacle than an asset."

"Because two congressmen were killed and the slain assassins had belonged to the agencies before being bodyguards for Pliny, the FBI and a couple of others will be investigating the case as well as the D.C. police. However, they don't know about the other murders or a possible connection."

"They'll find out and get suspicious anyway. They have computers too, and they'll learn about the incidents same as we did."

"I'm sure they will but I'm not assigning anyone else to this mission. To be honest, I'm not sure I can trust anyone in the FBI, CIA, BATF, DEA, NSA and so on. If this is a conspiracy, some highly-placed federal agents could be involved. I really don't know who to trust except you, Hal."

"I appreciate that. We'll try not to let you down. By the way, better be careful about the Secret Service agents assigned to protect you."

"Oh, I've thought about that," the President admitted. "I intend to keep familiar faces around me. The problem is, that might not be enough. Pliny thought he could trust Johnson and Sell too. If somebody is brainwashing protectors to turn on their employers, I might already have a murderer among my bodyguards.''

"I see your point. Still, best to stay with people you know."

"I think I'd feel better if you could provide some of your commandos to protect my family until this is over, but I know that's not your line of duty."

"Hopefully, we can take care of this matter before any more incidents occur."

"Yes, hopefully."

MORIHIRO KYKOSAWA PEERED through the metal guard of his face mask as his opponent approached. They both wore black *gi* uniforms with kendo torso protection and headgear. Kykosawa raised his *shinai* and advanced. His opponent attacked with his own mock sword. Kykosawa blocked with the split bamboo blade of his *shinai*.

His opponent attacked again, shoving down the stroke, attempting to force an opening for his blade. Kykosawa slipped his blade free. His adversary lost his balance for an instant, and Kykosawa quickly swung his blade, rapping the bamboo edge against the other man's helmet.

Both men stepped back. The loser bowed in silent acceptance. Kykosawa had won that round. They squared off again. His opponent's blade rose high in a fast effort to strike before Kykosawa could react. Bamboo clashed again. Kykosawa suddenly swung his blade across the other man's belly. He stepped forward, moving beside his opponent and chopped his sword again at kidney level.

"Omedeto gozaimas," his opponent stated. "Congratulations. You have won."

"*Arigato*," Kykosawa replied. "Thank you. You rely too much on strength for your attack. You need to remain fluid with a sword."

"*Hai*, Kykosawa-*san*. I'm afraid my skill with the sword will never match your own."

Kykosawa didn't respond. He knew that was true, but he didn't want to insult the other man or appear boastful. Yet, he didn't want to lie and give the man false hope. He removed his kendo helmet and crossed the dojo to place it on a dummy by the wall. Kykosawa set his sword on the rack and began shedding his protective gear. A buzzer sounded. Kykosawa reached inside his gym bag for his cellular phone. No larger than a pack of cigarettes, it was a state-of-the-art model designed and manufactured by Kumo Shima.

"*Moshi, moshi.*" He spoke into the phone with the traditional Japanese greeting.

"Garret Lynch is on line from New York," the voice of a secretary declared.

"Thank you," he said. "Put Mr. Lynch on."

He headed for a dressing room as he spoke. Kykosawa closed and locked the door for privacy.

"I understand you wanted to speak with me, Kykosawa."

Lynch's tone was arrogant and lacked respect. Kykosawa found the man's accent annoying and thought Lynch seemed to pronounce vowels with a slight whine.

"I appreciate you returning my call, Mr. Lynch. Have you had an opportunity to study the Kumo Shima products we discussed last week?"

"I've been busy," Lynch replied. "We have our own line and handle distribution for a number of companies. Goods from Taiwan and South Korea are less expensive to purchase, import and sell here in the States these days. You Japanese had a good thing going for a while, but I think you're beginning to slide down the economic food chain now."

"I think you exaggerate the situation," Kykosawa said. "You must also admit quality is important. Perhaps there are other markets with less costs involved, but none can match the quality of our Kumo Shima products."

"Hell," Lynch replied, "when people think of Oriental merchandise— Are we supposed to call you people Asian these days, or can we still call you Oriental? Never could keep track of that politically correct shit. Anyway, when people here in America think of stuff from your part of the world, they think cheap. All the pocket radios, little gadgets and other stuff people don't expect to last too long—we get all that from China. Cheapest market out there right now."

"Chinese." Kykosawa spoke the word as if an obscenity.

"Hey, in America everybody thinks you guys are all alike. Sorry to burst your bubble, but that's the way it is. They want quality, they want to feel good about themselves, they buy American. That's our quality line, pal. Made in the U.S. of A."

"I have heard your American products are really foreign imports altered to appear to be made in America with false labels and counterfeit casings."

"That's a lie, Kykosawa," Lynch declared, a sharp edge in his voice. "We have lawyers to handle slander against the company."

"I'm not accusing you of anything, Mr. Lynch," the Asian replied. "I simply mentioned a rumor that seems so widespread we have even heard of it here in Japan.

Certainly, there is no truth to such claims. Actually, the president of Chongwol Enterprises in Seoul is a friend of mine. I'm sure he can confirm that your trade with his company is perfectly honest and legal.''

Lynch didn't respond for several seconds. ''That shit might work with my partner, but I'm not impressed. I'm the boss here, Kykosawa. *Ichi-ban*. Understand? I make the final say, and Joel has to go along with it like everybody else.''

''That's why I'm speaking with you, Mr. Lynch. I'm already aware Joel Henly is impressed by the Kumo Shima products, and I had hoped you might share his opinion and decide to distribute our line of goods.''

''Hate to bust your rice bowl, but no chance.''

''I see,'' Kykosawa said with a sigh. ''Your chief of security was enrolled in our VR training program. Did he report an unfavorable view of our system?''

''He says it's okay,'' Lynch admitted. ''You want me to pull him from the course now? He's got one day left, but if you don't want him to complete the program...''

''Of course not, Mr. Lynch. That would be petty. Let him finish the program. It will help him do his job in the future.''

''You said we wouldn't have to pay for this. Change your mind about that?''

''I don't want a dime, Mr. Lynch.''

''That's mighty white of you, Kykosawa. That's a compliment.''

''You're too kind.''

''Well, this has been fun, but I've got work to do.''

''I understand. Thank you for your time.''

''Yeah,'' Lynch said. ''Don't take any wooden yen.''

The American hung up. Kykosawa switched off his cellular phone.

"Goodbye, you barbarian idiot," he said with a smile.

7

Leo Turrin poured some red wine into a glass, moved the bottle to another glass and looked at Mack Bolan. The Executioner shook his head. Turrin shrugged and set the bottle on the coffee table. The little Fed sunk into a chair and uttered a long sigh.

"Long day?" Bolan asked.

"Aren't they all?" Turrin replied as he sipped some wine. "But some are longer than others. I spent most of today with the D.C. cops and the FBI. Crazy stories about Sell and Johnson going nuts and killing a bunch of people. All pretty much the same. You know another cop died in the hospital?"

"I heard," Bolan said, nodding. "I read the files on those two. They don't fit the profile generally associated with people who lose their minds and go on a shooting spree. The fact they did it together makes it even more suspicious."

"Autopsies didn't find any evidence of narcotics that would cause this behavior. No brain tumors or other physical symptoms that might explain their actions. Everybody is scratching their heads and wondering what the hell happened. Frankly, I doubt we'd even be here if a couple congressmen hadn't been among the victims. This sort of thing has happened before, and we weren't called in to check on previous lunatics who gunned down a bunch of people.''

"Hal reckons these VIP security guys have been programmed to kill their bosses,'' Bolan said with a shrug. "This does seem to be a strange and alarming trend, but brainwashing isn't a simple process.''

"I wouldn't know,'' Turrin commented. "It's not my field.''

"Not mine either,'' the Executioner admitted. "I do know the efforts at behavior modification and reeducation programs carried out on prisoners of war required months or even years. Sell and Johnson didn't disappear for months prior to their shooting spree. Neither had Paul Greely at the Watley oil station or Dave Hull, the security expert who killed Brittly at the Chapman Robotics company.''

"Maybe somebody found a way to speed up the process. They didn't use drugs according to the autopsies. Maybe hypnosis?''

"You can't make somebody do something under hypnosis they wouldn't be willing to do because of moral and ethical reasons. I doubt all four of these guys were really cold-blooded killers who wanted to murder their employers and anybody else who got in their way. Actually, most efforts at brainwashing in the POW camps had limited success. A person's behavior, beliefs and ideals are formed by family, society, culture and experience that begins at birth. It's not so easy to reverse all that with counterconditioning techniques. Only certain types of personalities would respond.''

"Let me guess,'' Turrin began. "Guys who were products of lousy families who had no real sense of morality, patriotism or loyalty toward anything?''

"Pretty much,'' Bolan said with a nod. "The Communists tended to concentrate on brainwashing more than anyone else. The North Koreans and the North Vietnamese tried various methods to try to break POWs' will and reeducate them. Most American servicemen had been taught to hate communism even if they didn't really understand it or couldn't even give a half-ass definition what it meant. The majority didn't respond very well, and the few who did usually felt a lot of bitterness and resentment toward their own country, families and the government they felt had gotten them into a war and then let them down when they got captured.''

"I remember seeing some film footage of scrawny, sickly looking U.S. servicemen bowing in front of Commie officers and their flag," Turrin said. "They acted like zombies."

"Maybe they were zombies," Bolan said. "Voodoo priests called *houngans* have probably been producing zombies for centuries."

"Uh-huh," the little Fed grunted. "Aliens from outer space make duplicate human beings too. Maybe this is a plot by the Martians. Didn't they have a mind-control ray gun in Atlantis?"

"Laugh if you want, Leo," Bolan replied, "but there really are zombies in Haiti. There are well-documented cases of people declared dead by the doctors who examined them, yet later these 'dead' people are out of their graves and walking around. The *houngans* use a lot of herbs, roots, powders, toads, snakes, that sort of thing. A lot of these substances combined act as a magic formula. Apparently, they can produce a drug that causes a type of suspended animation in the victim that slows breathing and the heartbeat to a level it can't be detected. Ingredients for this are collected from various plants that grow in Haiti and poison from a species of puffer fish known as a sea toad. The victim is literally buried alive.''

"Jesus," Turrin rasped. "Don't they embalm corpses in Haiti?"

"I guess that's not a common practice there," Bolan replied. "The *houngan,* or whoever wanted the zombie curse carried out, digs up the dead person and revives him. Another drug is then used to break down the victim's willpower. One ingredient is a type of natural scopolamine used in truth serum. Of course, the victim is already traumatized by the experience and probably suffered a degree of brain damage from the poison and lack of oxygen. The victim is usually brought to a plantation and put to work as a zombie slave."

"This is for real?" Turrin asked. He seemed to hope Bolan wasn't serious, but realized he was. "Well, that's pretty freaky. It still doesn't explain the four guys who went nuts and did the killings we're looking into."

"No, it doesn't," Bolan confirmed. "It's just another possibility that can be ruled out in this case. Haitian zombies don't seem to be in very good shape, and I doubt they can skillfully handle a gun or display the quality of reflexes suggested by the Sell-Johnson incident."

Turrin sighed and reached for the wine bottle. The soldier understood his frustration. They were sitting in a motel room, spinning their mental wheels and getting nowhere. The police and the federal investigation agencies already involved were in the same situation. Stony Man had been called in by the President, but so far they didn't seem to be doing any better than anyone else.

A loud buzz sounded from a special laptop computer

on the desk in the room. Designed for Stony Man personnel in the field, it was a sophisticated model that linked them to the mighty mainframe at the Farm. Bolan headed for the unit before Turrin could rise from his seat. The Executioner saw the access code on the screen. A password appeared. For this occasion, "Europa" was used, which referred to one of four moons of Jupiter discovered by Galileo in 1610. Bolan punched in the name of the famous astronomer for the counterpassword.

Aaron Kurtzman came on-line. The screen displayed a real-time image of the computer expert sitting in his wheelchair, surrounded by computer banks, fax machines, color copiers and numerous other machines. Turrin joined Bolan by the desk.

"You two don't look so happy," Kurtzman remarked.

"If you're calling because we're late with a progress report, we haven't made any progress to report," Turrin stated.

The Executioner realized Kurtzman wouldn't have contacted them for something so trivial.

"What's up, Bear?"

"I came across a possible connection for the security gunmen gone berserk," Kurtzman replied. "Johnson and Sell had completed a special training course using advanced virtual reality techniques to develop their combat reflexes less than twelve hours before they arrived in D.C. to meet Congressman Pliny. Are you ready for the name of the company that provided this training program?"

"Not Kumo Shima?" the soldier asked, genuinely hoping that wouldn't be the answer.

"Afraid so," Kurtzman said. "Pliny's bodyguards

took the course at the Kumo Shima base in Texas. David Hull also graduated from the VR training the day before he killed Brittly at Chapman Robotics. Paul Greely was one of the first to take the Kumo Shima course. That was about forty-eight hours before he returned to Alaska.''

"What's this Kumo Shima business?" Turrin asked. "Sounds like something you'd order in a sushi bar."

"I'll explain later," Bolan told him. "Do you have a list of everyone who signed up for this VR training course?"

"Not a complete list," Kurtzman answered. "Kumo Shima has tight security. Tapping into their computer system is tougher than getting access to the CIA. The sons of bitches know their high-tech hardware. They probably store their most confidential data separately from the mainframe so we can't access it. I found out about the four triggermen by checking their records and the companies they worked for, not from Kumo Shima."

"What about airline records of flights made by experts in security professions who recently traveled to Dallas for short-term business?" Bolan asked.

Kurtzman nodded and said, "That's how we started tracking down the connection to begin with. I've got a list of names of professional bodyguards, security chiefs, federal officers and policemen. Some attended the course and some might have. We're still working on confirmations. We do have one definite candidate for a walking time bomb who is on his way home from Texas."

"You mean he's flying back as we speak?" Bolan asked.

"He might be landing in New York right now," Kurtzman answered.

"His name is Greg Olson, security head for Lynch-Henly Unlimited. That's a marketing outfit that specializes in computer hardware and distribution of various electronic items, including a lot of imports from the Far East. Still, they haven't done much business with Japan lately. After the economy in Japan took a nosedive a few years ago, Lynch-Henly has concentrated on markets from Taiwan, Korea and China."

"Why the hell would anybody want to kill the head of a computer marketing agency?" Turrin wondered aloud.

"Why kill the head of a robotics company?" Bolan replied. "Where is this company located?"

"Manhattan," Kurtzman answered. "I'll fax you guys the data we have so far. By the way, Olson is an ex-Marine, used to have an intelligence military occupational specialty and scored high on marksmanship, survival skills and hand-to-hand combat. Tough customer. He also has a pistol permit for New York and carries a Heckler & Koch 9 mm. You might want to keep that in mind if you go up against him, Striker."

"Thanks for the info," Bolan replied. "Jack has a Bell chopper at an airstrip outside of D.C. It's short range for a flight to New York, and it would require some stops for fuel along the way. He might need to rent a small plane, and there could be a hassle about getting a flight charter and permission to take off on short notice."

"We can pull the necessary strings with the FAA," Kurtzman assured him.

"Okay," the soldier said. "I'm on my way as soon as you fax the details. What about Able Team?"

"They're supposed to return today," Kurtzman stated. "We haven't been in touch with them since they called via telephone to a secure linkup line. They didn't take a laptop to Texas. Figured it would draw too much attention, and we didn't think anything like this would happen."

"You mean Able Team was down there with the people who are programming these killers?" Turrin asked with astonishment. "You don't think they could have been turned?"

"I think we'd better not take any chances," Bolan replied. "They didn't take the laptop, but I assume they're armed."

"They had cover names, as government agents, and federal pistol permits," Kurtzman answered. "They'll be carrying their handguns. Kissinger is preparing a reception committee for when they arrive."

"Able Team is good," the Executioner commented. "Very good. The Cowboy had better be careful."

"He knows that," Kurtzman said, nodding, "but they're our guys, Striker. Hell, they're your friends. You and Able Team go back a long way. Pol and Gadgets served with you in the Army."

"I know that," Bolan stated, his voice sharper than he intended. "I'm not suggesting they be shot on sight, but I also appreciate their skill and experience. If Able Team goes crazy, they could make the Johnson-Sell shooting spree look like a Sunday picnic."

"Jesus," Turrin remarked, "we're talking about Able Team. How the hell could anybody turn them against us in less than a week?"

"We don't know that happened," Kurtzman told him. "Other people have taken the Kumo Shima course without going nuts. The guys who lost it all seem to have had particular targets. They were bodyguards or security heads for VIPs known to the public. They were probably chosen to take out their bosses. Other cops and federal agents might just go through the VR training so they can spread the word about how great it is. Remember how Kissinger was impressed by the demo he attended?''

"Yeah," the Executioner agreed. "They must have a pretty impressive system set up if they can produce that type of rapid brainwashing."

"Maybe that's what's going on," Kurtzman said. "Still, I never heard of anything like this before. I've been trying to get information on Kumo Shima and the people involved."

"First things first, Aaron," Bolan insisted. "We all have work to do, and none of us have time to spare."

"Right," Kurtzman replied. "I'm faxing that material to you now. There's some information about an FBI district officer in New York you can contact to cut through the red tape when you arrive. Don't forget what I said about Olson. Don't underestimate the guy."

"I never underestimate anyone."

Copies of data sheets and photographs appeared on the laptop. Bolan reached for his shoulder holster and slipped into the harness. The Beretta 93-R was once again in its familiar position under his arm.

"This stuff is too much for me," Turrin commented, shaking his head. "We're talking about brainwashing and killers, and now it's all linked to glorified video games."

"Real people are getting killed and real people are responsible for it," the Executioner replied. "This isn't a game, Leo, but it sure as hell has some deadly players."

8

Rosario Blancanales gazed out the window of the 747. He saw only sky and clouds of various forms. A shape with a long base, mounted with white puffs and tall swirls that drifted into faded peaks, caught his eye. An island of clouds. Kumo Shima.

"Well," Hermann Schwarz said as he placed a computer magazine on his tray, "I expected that VR technology to be pretty good to earn such raves from the Cowboy, but it was even more impressive than I anticipated."

Carl Lyons glanced at his fellow Able Team commandos. He squeezed a tennis ball in his big fist as he checked the aisle to be certain no one was close enough to eavesdrop on their conversation. Accustomed to danger, he also scanned the seats for anyone who appeared suspicious. After years in law enforcement and antiterrorist assignments, Lyons half expected to encounter skyjackers every time he set foot in a commercial aircraft.

"Yeah," he said, "it was almost too real. I felt like I was in a real battlefield during the final session. I even got into hand-to-hand with the last opponent. It really felt like the guy grabbed my wrist to hold back my gun while trying to stick me with a knife. It felt like I really grabbed him, too. If I didn't know better, I would have sworn I wrapped an arm around a living man's neck, brought him down to the floor and twisted his head until I heard bone crunch. When they can make something like that seem so real...it's kind of creepy.''

A flight attendant rolled her cart to their section. She asked if they wanted coffee, tea or soda. Each man made his selection, then waited until she moved on.

"I wouldn't say it was creepy," Schwarz stated. "Oh, the simulated realism is disarming and stressful, but it's supposed to reproduce genuine combat situations as accurately as possible. The question is, should Stony Man use the Kumo Shima program as an addition to training in the future?"

"No," Blancanales declared. "I don't think we should."

The man's expression was serious. His fingers tapped the rock maple shaft of his cane as he looked at his partners.

"There's something wrong with the VR program we attended," he insisted. "I can't quite explain what it is, but I have a gut feeling that those people are up to something."

"They're in business to make a profit," Schwarz said with a shrug. "A lot of business reps are sort of sleazy characters. Yong seemed a little insincere when he talked about lofty motives, but that doesn't mean there's anything sinister involved."

"Maybe," Lyons allowed, "but I know what Pol means. My instincts tell me there's something fishy about Kumo Shima. One thing that bothered me is I felt like a human lab rat. They kept us in the compound the whole time. Fed us meals, put us through the VR paces and then packed us off to our rooms to sleep and get up for more of the same.''

"They don't have a compound," Schwarz said. "It's a research and training center. Just a building, Carl. Yong never said we couldn't leave anytime we wanted. They didn't lock the doors at night or post guards outside our rooms."

"Those sessions were mentally and emotionally exhausting and even physically demanding to a degree," Blancanales stated. "No one felt like going out on the town for some Dallas nightlife after spending the day in simulated combat situations that were so real you could smell the VR blood on your clothes."

"It got a little rough in the end," Schwarz had to confess. "Still, it was supposed to, Pol. Rooms were provided because they said it would be exhausting. I'm still not convinced there's anything odd about the setup. Hell, they didn't even ask us to check our guns. If they were up to anything illegal or subversive, they wouldn't have let us be armed and able to wander around the place."

"We don't know if they would've let us snoop around," Lyons commented. "We were too worn out to do anything but eat and sleep. Come to think of it, that's kind of weird. I'm used to pumping iron two hours a day, and I try to run at least two miles every morning, but those sessions wiped me out."

"Exactly," Blancanales agreed. "We've all been in genuine combat numerous times in the past. Did you ever feel so spent afterward? Isn't it odd that simulated combat would be more demanding than the real thing?"

"Perhaps in some ways the VR version is more intense," Schwarz suggested. "It's rather like being placed in an alien environment. You never know what might happen. In virtual reality, they can have enemies materialize from thin air or have opponents shoot fire out their eyes or launch ice daggers from their navels.''

"I sort of expected that kind of nonsense when I first arrived," Lyons said. "But after a taste of how realistic the system was, I didn't figure they'd throw in a flying gorilla with a ray gun."

Schwarz sighed. He loved high-tech devices and electronic contraptions. His skill and interest in these fields had earned him the nickname "Gadgets" long before he joined Stony Man. Schwarz was more inclined to embrace an advanced technology than his partners.

"Okay," he began. "I doubt the VR program caused some sort of serious mental fatigue that could hurt our performance in the field. Probably just the opposite. The idea is to improve our reflexes for actual combat. However, I will agree that the Farm should investigate the Kumo Shima project to a greater degree before they decide to either use the system for training or attempt to develop something like it on our own."

"Sounds reasonable to me," Lyons agreed. "What do you think, Pol?"

Blancanales had earned his nickname as "Politician" or "Pol" because he had a way with people. He could charm and disarm with words. The Hispanic commando specialized in negotiating compromises that would satisfy everyone involved. He thoughtfully tapped a finger along the shaft of his cane and glanced out the window at the clouds.

"Yeah," he replied, "I guess so. I still think there's something disturbing about the Kumo Shima project, but that might be foolishness on my part."

"Some people call it future shock," Schwarz explained. "New technology can seem to be too much to handle, arriving faster than anyone expects it. Try looking at it as changes that offer new opportunities and challenges. That's how you make the future more exciting than frightening.''

"Maybe it's both," Blancanales replied.

"It always has been," Lyons added with a shrug.

Blancanales wasn't satisfied with Gadgets's explanation, but he realized he didn't have logical grounds to debate the issue. He also couldn't explain a strange sense of dread that nagged him as they headed back for Stony Man Farm.

SPECIAL AGENT BRYANT GRUNDY wasn't very happy about being ordered to meet with the mysterious Michael Belasko. He was probably even less pleased to discover Belasko was in charge and intended to march into Lynch-Henly Unlimited to apprehend the chief of security.

Grundy drove the black sedan through the dense traffic along Broadway. The streets of Manhattan were always frantic with thousands of vehicles crammed into the multilanes. Drivers honked horns, screamed, cursed and generally behaved like escapees from a mental ward.

They were trapped in a midday rush. Bolan couldn't imagine why anyone would venture onto the streets in this madness just to have lunch, but to some people lunch was an opportunity to conduct business with clients softened up with a few martinis. The soldier was content to let Grundy drive.

Bolan had never been fond of driving in New York City. The Fed's expression seemed tense. Bolan wasn't sure if that was because of traffic or Grundy was annoyed that he had to take orders from the Executioner.

"You know the Lynch-Henly company is a big outfit with a lot of influence across the United States," Grundy said, eyes fixed on the windshield as he spoke. "In fact they have influence in other countries, as well. Major distributors and importers. Lots of friends in high places, including government officials and politicians, as well as business and industry."

"That's fascinating," Bolan said dryly. "We're not going to harass the CEOs or stir up any more fuss than necessary. We'll just go in and explain we need to meet with their security chief, Mr. Olson."

"And he'll just come along quietly with us?" Grundy asked with a frown. "You said the guy is a potential time bomb. I heard about those crazy bastards who turned on two congressmen and wasted a bunch of cops. If Olson even twitches a finger toward a gun…"

"We'll bear in mind he might be dangerous," the soldier assured him, "but he might not turn violent unless he sees the person or persons he intends to assassinate."

"What?" Grundy asked with surprise. "Are you serious? Sounds like some sort of far-fetched crap from a bad movie. Next thing you'll tell me is the son of a bitch is a cyborg."

"Just back me up, Grundy," Bolan told him. "Hopefully, we can just escort him from the building with no trouble, get him to go to your station and detain him long enough to determine if there's something wrong with him."

"You're not even sure he's really a nutcase," Grundy said with disgust. "I swear, when I get back I'm calling the Bureau and requesting a complete investigation of you and your source of authority. This

White House authority business sounded peculiar to me from the start.''

"You can call anybody you want after we take care of Olson. Isn't that our turn up ahead?''

"Forty-fifth Street,'' Grundy said with a nod. "Almost there.''

He turned right at the corner. Soon they approached the parking lot of a large office building of concrete and glass. The structure housed several company headquarters, including Lynch-Henly Unlimited. Grundy paid an attendant ten dollars to use a visitor parking space protected by security guards to prevent the vehicle from being stolen or vandalized.

"The mayor keeps telling everybody the crime rate is going down,'' Grundy commented as he shut off the engine, "but the city still feels like a war zone.''

"Every place is,'' Bolan remarked.

They entered the lobby. Guards watched them from desk stations with little interest. Bolan and Grundy didn't match the guards' preconceived notions of criminals or terrorists. No one asked who they were or why they were there until Grundy flashed his ID.

"FBI,'' he announced. "How do we get to the Lynch-Henly offices as fast as possible?''

"What's this about?''

"We just need to talk to somebody, but we're in a hurry.''

"Tenth floor,'' the guard stated. "They got the whole tenth floor.''

Bolan and Grundy headed for the elevators. The soldier didn't like traveling in elevator cars. A lift shaft was too easy to sabotage. They entered the elevator and Bolan punched the button for the tenth floor.

Grundy reached inside his jacket and drew a .38 Special from a belly holster. He opened the cylinder and stared at the cartridges in the chambers. The Fed closed the cylinder and reholstered the revolver. Bolan wondered if the guy really had to check the gun to be sure it was loaded or if this was some sort of macho display for the Executioner's benefit. Either way, it didn't make a favorable impression on Bolan.

The doors opened, and they approached another guard station. Unlike the blue-clad security for the building in general, Lynch-Henly guards wore black trousers and white short-sleeve shirts. Badges labeled them as rent-a-cops and shoulder patches bore the letters LHU. A rack behind the desk held a trio of nightsticks and walkie-talkies.

A heavyset black man looked at the pair and frowned. He moved from the desk to step closer. Bolan noticed the guy wore a belt ring for a baton but didn't carry a side arm.

"You two FBI?" he asked.

"The guy must have called from downstairs, huh?" Grundy said as he got out his ID.

"Yeah," the guard replied. "If I had telepathy, I doubt I'd be working here. What can we do for you?"

"We need to speak with your boss," the Fed stated. "That is to say, Security Chief Olson. Is he in his office?"

"He just got back from out of state and said he wanted to report directly to Mr. Lynch and Mr. Henly."

"Where are they?" Bolan asked, his tone as hard as steel.

"Uh, past the secretary pool. The offices are labeled, but they might be meeting in the conference room."

The Executioner took off beyond the station, followed by Grundy, marching into the secretary pool.

The secretaries stared up at the big, rugged man dressed in black and the FBI agent clad in the unofficial federal uniform of a single-breasted suit, dress shirt and necktie. Obviously, they didn't resemble the typical clientele at Lynch-Henly Unlimited.

Bolan glanced around as he strode across the room. The names of the presidents of the company identified their offices. The last door probably led to the conference room.

The door opened as Bolan approached. A short, portly man gazed up at him through wire-rimmed glasses. He shuffled backward, startled. Another figure appeared behind him. The second man was taller, more fit and didn't appear to be accustomed to backing down from anyone. Bolan recognized the lantern jaw, thin lips and narrow nose beneath blond hair clipped in a crew cut. The Executioner had seen the face in a faxed copy of Olson's file.

"What's...uh..." the portly man began in an unsteady voice. "May I help you, gentlemen?"

He seemed nervous, perhaps because Grundy looked like a federal agent. The guy probably thought they were from the Better Business Bureau or the IRS.

"Special Agent Grundy with the FBI," the Fed announced. "And this is Agent Belasko."

"Maybe I should talk to them, Mr. Henly," the big blond guy volunteered in a voice as gruff as one might expect from an ex-Marine.

Olson emerged from the conference room. He was nearly as tall as Bolan, and the padded shoulders of his sports coat made him look like a football player. Olson barely glanced at Grundy as he turned his attention to the Executioner. Bolan hadn't flashed any ID or said a word, but the veteran military man recognized a fellow soldier.

"I'm in charge of security here," he announced. "What's this about?"

"Actually," Grundy began, "we need to speak with you, Mr. Olson. You're not in any trouble or anything like that, but we do want to talk about this in a secure and confidential setting."

"What the hell do you mean by 'this'?" Olson demanded.

"It concerns the Kumo Shima training program you just attended in Texas," Bolan explained. "Because a number of federal agents are scheduled to attend, we'd appreciate some inside information about the project from a qualified observer."

"I was told there were already some Feds attending the program," Olson remarked.

"Well, I don't understand why you have to take our head of security off for some sort of inquisition when you have officers of the federal government already at this VR training site," Henly added. "But you can use our conference room or perhaps my office."

"That's kind of you, Mr. Henly," Grundy replied.

He glanced at Bolan and whispered, "You are aware this is Mr. Henly? One of the company presidents?"

Bolan nodded. Grundy mentioned that because Olson had shown no hostile behavior near his boss. Perhaps the security head wasn't a threat to his employers.

"I would like to talk with Mr. Lynch before we start a detailed conversation," Olson stated. "The arrangements to go to Kumo Shima had been made by him, and he did want me to tell him about it as soon as possible."

"Lynch was on the phone making a conference call

to some overseas clients," Henly informed Bolan. "He should be finished soon. Can't you wait a half hour or so to give Olson a chance to talk to my partner?"

"We'd like to get this over with," Bolan explained. "This is important. There are matters of national security involved. Right now, I can't say more than that."

"National security?" Olson asked with surprise. "How does a program centered on virtual reality simulations have anything to do with national security?"

"We really can't talk about that here," Grundy said. "Please come with us, and we'll explain what we can."

"Wait a minute," Henly began. "This business seems a little strange to me, too. Show me some ID. I want to be sure you men are really FBI."

Grundy fished out his folder once more. Bolan also got out his Belasko ID. Henly took a notepad and pen from his secretary's desk to jot down the numbers on their cards. Obviously, he didn't intend to let them leave with Olson until he called the FBI district office to confirm they were genuine.

"What the hell is going on?" a voice demanded.

They turned to see a man at the threshold to Lynch's office. The man's lean face seemed hard. His lips were drawn tight across capped teeth, eyes narrowed and brow wrinkled in an expression of seething anger. Lynch didn't like anything to happen in his domain without his approval, and he immediately realized the scene he encountered would challenge his control.

"Bastard!" Olson exclaimed as he lunged forward.

The security chief drew his pistol from the holster under his jacket as he spoke, pointed it at Lynch and pulled the trigger without hesitation. Two shots rang out within the confines of the secretary pool. Grundy was closer to Olson and managed to reach him before

Bolan, effectively blocking the Executioner in the process.

Screams and gasps sounded around them from the horrified spectators. Lynch collapsed by the door to his office while Grundy made a desperate grab for Olson's gun. The burly security chief bent an elbow and slammed it into the point of Grundy's chin. The FBI agent fell backward, a groan barely detected above the snapping of his teeth.

Bolan moved in like a shark. He approached from a swift semicircle, reaching Olson. His right hand closed on the man's pistol, and he jammed his thumb into the back of the gunman's fist. Bolan's left hand grabbed the guy's wrist, shoving the captive arm high to point the weapon away from the bystanders.

Olson triggered another round. The pistol jerked in their collective grip, but Bolan held on, aware the bullet had blasted into the ceiling.

The Executioner stomped his boot heel into his opponent's kneecap as he twisted Olson's hand and wrist. Bolan pushed hard with both hands to bend the gunman's wrist more than the joint was designed to handle. Bone crunched. Olson cried out in a tone that expressed more anger than pain, but his hand still opened to drop the pistol.

Despite the pain and disabled wrist, Olson suddenly lashed out with his other hand. That caused more bone to crack in the captive wrist, but the man seemed oblivious as he thrust a heel-of-the-palm stroke to Bolan's chest. The blow propelled both men into a desk. The soldier found himself sprawled across the desktop with Olson on his chest. The security chief's face contorted with rage, eyes ablaze with demented fury as he tried to pin Bolan with his weight and jam a forearm across the Executioner's throat.

Bolan pushed the arm as best he could, only to realize Olson had the advantage. The guy could use all of his weight to push down while the soldier could push back with just his arms. He knew he had to act quickly before his adversary crushed his windpipe. Bolan braced himself with his back and shoulders on the desktop and swung a leg high, thrusting it across Olson's chest and face.

The Executioner pressed the leg under Olson's chin. His thigh found the man's throat as he bent his knee to wrap the calf around the back of his opponent's neck. Aware a person's leg was stronger than an arm, Bolan twisted a hip, pulling his opponent off with the leg-locked grip around Olson's neck. The security man was suddenly yanked backward into the edge of the desk. Bolan knew he couldn't hold on to his adversary with just the leg-lock before the guy would counterattack and throw him off balance. He released the guy quickly and slammed a hard punch to Olson's jaw before the man could respond.

The Executioner pushed away from the desk and turned to face his opponent. Olson advanced slowly, his body running out of whatever maniacal energy powered it regardless of pain or injury. The warrior feinted with his right hand and jabbed his left fist into Olson's chin. He followed with a right cross. The security chief staggered, and Bolan swung a leg to simply trip the man and dump him on the carpet.

"Hold it!" a voice ordered.

Bolan glanced away from his dazed opponent on the floor to see the two security guards advance. Armed only with batons, they had waited until they were sure no more shots would be fired before they moved in. The secretaries had retreated to their desks for cover, shocked by the unexpected violence and bloodshed.

Olson began to rise. Blood dripped from his nostrils and mouth, and his right hand dangled from his broken wrist. Lynch lay motionless, his shirt stained red at the center of his chest. There was a slim chance he was alive.

"What the hell is going on?" the black guard demanded. "Who shot Mr. Lynch?"

Before anyone could answer, Olson suddenly bolted for the nearest window, diving through it without hesitation. Glass shattered and the framework gave way. The security chief plunged from view, landing seconds later on the pavement ten stories below.

"Oh, my God," Henly rasped as he stared at the broken window frame.

Grundy got to his feet, a hand braced on his sore jaw. He started to speak, coughed and spit out a broken piece of tooth with a glob of blood. He cursed softly and turned to face Bolan.

"Guess you were right," he muttered. "Happy?"

"I'm a long way from being happy, Grundy," the soldier replied. "We've got to get out of here."

"Like hell you will!" the guard declared. "We've got a murder-suicide here, and the cops are going to want some answers."

"You've got a room full of witnesses for the police," Bolan replied. "They can tell you Olson killed Lynch, and everybody saw him dive out that window. We have to get to the airport as fast as possible. I have to leave. You can tell the cops to contact Grundy at the FBI office later today."

"Why do we have to rush to the airport?" the Fed asked, as surprised as the others in the room.

"Because you can get me there faster than I could on my own," Bolan stated. "And I have to get on that plane with my partner because we need to get to another state pronto."

"What do you mean?" Grundy insisted.

"I mean something like this might happen again, and we have to try to stop it. Now, let's go."

9

Huntington Wethers studied the radar screen as he sat at his station in the Stony Man computer center. A tall African-American and former college professor, Wethers was acknowledged as one of the top experts in cybernetics in the state of California, if not the entire country. He had taught the subject at Berkeley but became disillusioned with his role as an educator. Too many students seemed motivated only by goals of high financial profits.

They wanted to be accountants, stockbrokers, video-game designers and special-effects animation experts in Hollywood. Wethers was disappointed most had little interest in developing and improving computer technology. He believed the computer age should offer more jobs, more comforts and a better standard of living for everyone.

Wethers had accepted the offer to join Stony Man Farm because it allowed him to use his skills and knowledge to help advance cybernetics and serve the interests of the world in a way he had never expected—fighting terrorism, crime and international conspiracies from a computer terminal was a new and exciting experience for him. He was also pleased to work with Aaron Kurtzman and the other members of the Stony Man Farm.

The combination of a covert life of computerized intrigue and a type of public service proved to be an agreeable choice for Wethers. He had never really been a man of action in the sense of a soldier, a policeman or an adventurer. The computer center at Stony Man seemed to be the best place for him to carry out his contribution to the battle against physical evil in a confused and dangerous world. He hadn't expected the Farm itself might become a combat zone.

Wethers realized the Stony Man base had been attacked before he joined the team. Security had been improved to protect the Farm from detection and invasion by enemy forces. But they had never expected a threat from their own people.

The communications system announced someone online with the special secure transceiver network to the mainframe. Akira Tokaido, another member of the cybernetics crew, watched the terminal as access codes and passwords confirmed the call came from Mack Bolan. The young Japanese-American removed the earphones to his portable CD player as the Executioner's head and shoulders appeared on the screen.

"Hello, Striker," Tokaido greeted. "Heard about what happened in New York. A tap into the NYPD computers told us Olson killed Lynch and took a swan dive out a window. Cops want to talk to Belasko, you know. The FBI is angry you took off."

"We'll square things for Grundy later," Bolan replied. "The guy doesn't deserve to get burned because we brought him into this. Any word on Able Team?"

"Not really," the technician answered. "They didn't take a laptop with them to Texas. Figured they wouldn't need it for a simple training program, and a high-tech contraption like that might attract more attention and suspicion than necessary. That was the logic at the time. It doesn't seem so smart now.''

"Hindsight would be great if it was useful. They didn't even use a phone link?''

"Nope," Tokaido said. "We know they caught their flight from Texas to Virginia. We got that data from airport computers. It seems we've been better at communicating with machines than people. Able Team arrived in Virginia, and the guys are on their way here.''

"I thought they'd wait at the airport for Grimaldi.''

"They had expected him to be waiting for them. Of course, Jack is with you. Now, we keep a couple choppers in hangars at more than one airport just in case. Well, you know both Lyons and Gadgets are qualified helicopter pilots.''

"Great. So they checked out a chopper and they're heading home. Have they made radio contact yet?''

"No," Tokaido said with a sigh, "but we're monitoring both radio and radar. Everybody here is on pins and needles waiting for them. Maybe we're worrying without good cause. Not all the Kumo Shima subjects have turned homicidal.''

"Yeah," Bolan replied. "Olson seemed okay until he saw Lynch. He didn't act hostile toward Henly and didn't seem upset when Grundy and I showed up. The moment he set eyes on Lynch he pulled a gun and started shooting. Also, he seemed almost immune to pain. You guys might keep that in mind when Able Team arrives.''

"Cowboy is in charge of that," Tokaido stated. "He's got the blacksuits together and they're ready.''

"I've known those three guys for a long time. Don't count on anybody ever being ready for them. They're three of the best skilled and most resourceful fighting men in the world.''

"Cowboy is no slouch either. He hopes to meet them at the chopper pad and try to take them into custody with as little fuss as possible. If they do turn violent, Cowboy and his men are decked out in riot gear and armed with nonlethal weapons so they can capture the guys without having to hurt them.''

"The feeling might not be mutual,'' Bolan commented. "Where's Aaron?''

"Call of nature. He's in the bathroom. Considering how much of that awful black crap he calls coffee he drinks, I'm surprised he isn't there more often.''

"Thanks for sharing that information. What about Hal and Barbara?''

"They're in the War Room,'' Tokaido replied. "I can patch you through....''

"That's okay,'' Bolan assured him. "You can let him know Jack and I reached Virginia and we're on our way. Able Team doesn't have much of a head start. Jack's a hell of a pilot, but even he can't make this helicopter fly any faster than it is designed for. We should get there in about half an hour.''

"Able will be here before that.''

"Well, suggest to Hal that he'd better stay in the War Room and out of sight of Able Team when they get there. If they've been programmed, the enemy probably wasn't able to learn the exact identity of a target so they might be set to go into action only if they see their chief commander.''

"We kind of figured that out already based on what information we've been able to gather so far.''

Huntington Wethers stepped away from the radar unit. He turned to Tokaido and the image of Bolan on the screen. With a dignified nod of greeting to the soldier, Wethers spoke in a solemn tone.

"I have Able Team on radar. They'll be here soon."

HAL BROGNOLA SLID OPEN a desk drawer and reached for a box of cigars. He glanced at the snub-nosed .38 Smith & Wesson revolver in a clip-on holster by the box. The big Fed knew he ought to carry the gun, but he probably wouldn't need it. Kissinger and his men had set up defenses with a solid plan to apprehend Able Team before any problems could occur. It was hard to imagine anyone getting past them, even three men as well trained and skilled as Able Team.

Yet, it wasn't impossible. Brognola knew better than to underestimate the commando trio. He never thought he might be faced with the necessity of killing one or more of his most trusted Stony Man personnel. Maybe the world really was insane. Brognola removed two cigars from the box, left the .38 in the drawer and closed it.

Barbara Price stood by the table at the War Room and gazed at the radar scan from the computer center, confirming the chopper was coming in fast. Price held a Nova stun gun in one hand and tapped it thoughtfully in the open palm of the other. Brognola stuck the cigars in his pocket as he advanced.

"I can't believe we're waiting for Able Team as if they were an invading force," Price remarked.

"If they have been brainwashed, they're potentially more dangerous than any enemy that has previously attacked the Farm," Brognola commented. "They know the area, codes to get into buildings, security systems—where we're most vulnerable."

"How could anyone brainwash Carl, Gadgets and

Pol in less than four days?'' Price asked and shook her head. ''They have strong personalities and loyalties. It just doesn't seem possible.''

''Let's hope it isn't, and we're worrying about something that won't happen,'' the big Fed replied.

A window materialized on screen, and Aaron Kurtzman appeared. His big shoulders hunched forward as he leaned over a keyboard to the horseshoe-shaped cockpit where he ruled as supreme master of the computer wizardry of Stony Man.

''Hal,'' Kurtzman began, ''Lyons is on the radio. He requested permission to land. Do we give it to him or stall?''

''Tell him yes,'' Brognola answered. ''If we don't let them land, they'll eventually set down somewhere outside the Farm and then we'll have to cope with whatever sort of sneak attack they might come up with. Better if we let them land on the helipad and try to take them as quickly and gently as possible.''

''Right. Striker called in. Akira told him about our situation. He and Jack are headed this way.''

''Wish they were here already. I don't imagine Striker happened to learn anything that will help with this possible attack by Able Team?''

''He had sound advice,'' Kurtzman answered. ''Pretty much common sense that we've managed to figure out on our own. It seemed to emphasize that you should stay out of sight for now. And nobody better underestimate Able Team.''

''I don't think anybody will. I'm going to put Cowboy on-line.''

Brognola pressed buttons on his keyboard. A second window appeared on-screen next to Kurtzman while the radar scan with a white blimp continued to dominate the background. Surveillance cameras outside the building transmitted real-time video of Kissinger and a dozen blacksuits. Clad in dark uniforms, riot helmets and flak vests, they resembled a unit of SWAT officers prepared to take on a crisis.

Kissinger was recognizable due to his size. He was the biggest guy in the group. Some of the troops carried bullet-resistant shields. All packed stun guns of one type or another. Several had rubber batons. A device that resembled a cut-down motor launcher stood near the Stony Man armorer. Brognola wasn't sure what it was, but assumed Kissinger had it on hand for a good reason.

"Heads up, John," the big Fed announced. "Able will be here soon. They just requested permission to land."

"The fact they asked might be a good sign," Kissinger replied through a throat mike.

They had no visual contact with Kissinger aside from the spy cameras, but he could communicate through a two-way radio built into the helmet. He carried a contraption that resembled a sawed-off single-barrel shotgun. Brognola recognized it as a type of stun gun that fired a bean-bag projectile designed to take down an opponent with a long-range knockout punch. Others in his group had Taser stun guns or modified cattle prods.

"This might be a bad time to bring this up," Brognola began, "but that chopper they got at the airport isn't armed, is it?"

"We wouldn't leave a gunship equipped with rockets and mounted machine guns in a civilian hangar," Kissinger replied. "It's not very likely Able Team could have supplied it with arms on their own. Not this quickly at least. I doubt they smuggled a .30 cal through airport security. Of course, they could have used something easy to improvise like bottle bombs or Molotov cocktails.''

"Great," Brognola muttered. "I knew I shouldn't have brought this up."

"Hopefully, they won't attempt an attack from the air. They probably couldn't do much damage that way. Our buildings are constructed to endure a lot of explosive punishment. Of course, if that happens we won't have any choice except to bring them down with an antiaircraft gun. If we blow them out of the sky, there won't be any survivors.''

"I realize that," the big Fed said grimly. "If they land on the pad?"

''No Jeep will meet them. They'll have to start walking to the main house, and we'll stop them before they reach you."

''They're going to get suspicious when they see you guys dressed in riot gear.''

"We don't intend to advertise," Kissinger assured him. "We'll hide in bushes and grassy knolls on both sides of the path to the house, then we'll close in around them. I'll announce who we are in case Able hasn't been brainwashed, and then we can try to do everything in a peaceful and civilized manner. If not, we'll try to handle it without anybody getting hurt. Able Team is probably armed with only pistols. Our shields and body armor will protect us while we get close enough to take them with nonlethal weaponry.''

"You sure that'll work?"

"They're three damn tough guys," Kissinger mused, "especially Carl. Still, even he'll go down if we hit him with enough electrical shocks, spray him with pepper spray and pound him with rubber batons a few times."

"You sound confident."

"Well, if there's no other choice, I'm also packing a .44 Magnum. I sure hope it won't come to that."

"Me, too," the big Fed agreed.

"With a little luck everything will be okay, Hal."

"We could do with some luck."

"I'm sure sorry I encouraged you to send Able Team to that Kumo Shima course," Kissinger admitted. "I sort of feel like this is partly my fault."

"Hell, there was no way you could have guessed something like this would happen," Brognola assured him. "If Able Team has been programmed against us, the bastards who did it are to blame. Not you."

"But I shouldn't have been so eager to send them without making absolutely sure the Kumo Shima outfit was okay. I can't change what already happened, so I'll try to make up for it now."

"Just stay professional and not emotional, John," the big Fed urged.

Brognola glanced away from the screen and looked at Price. Her expression remained calm, but he saw the concern in her eyes and the nervous gesture with the Nova in her hand.

"You know you have to get close to use that thing," he commented. "It's not much good against an opponent with a gun."

"The Nova stun gun uses nonlethal electricity," Price replied, aware Brognola already knew that fact. "Thousands of volts, but no amps. It'll be a better way for me to try to subdue a big strong man than trying to do it with my bare hands."

"Cowboy will take care of it before anybody can

reach the building anyway," Brognola commented. "You won't need the Nova."

"Right," Price said without conviction. "Want me to get one for you...just in case?"

"I think I'll get a Taser instead," Brognola replied. "It uses nonlethal electricity, too, and it has a longer reach—"

His sentence ended abruptly when the radar scanner vanished from the wall screen, replaced by a video display from another surveillance camera. A helicopter appeared in the blue-and-white sky. It approached the Farm and began to descend.

"This is it," Brognola remarked, a trace of tension in his voice.

The chopper moved across the sky and dipped below a line of treetops. Brognola frowned, aware the craft wasn't headed toward the helipad. It appeared to be flying low at the southeast corner of the Farm.

"Hal?" Kissinger's voice spoke from the receiver.

"I know," Brognola replied. "The camera angle is blocked by trees. Can you see the chopper?"

"Not from here," Kissinger replied, "but it was coming down fast and seemed to weave a lot. Almost like it was out of control."

Suddenly, an explosion sounded from the receiver and Brognola watched the wall screen. Flames appeared, burning the tree branches like a giant fireball. The big Fed sucked in a tense breath, and Price gasped.

"Oh, God! They've crashed!"

10

Kissinger jumped into the passenger seat of a Jeep as one of his men slid behind the wheel. Other members of the defense unit climbed into their vehicles, following the armorer's lead. Four Jeeps bolted south toward the smoke and fire of the fallen helicopter.

"You think any of them are still alive?" the driver asked, voice muffled by the clear plastic visor of his helmet.

"We'll find out," Kissinger replied curtly. "What the hell happened?"

The two-way radio in his helmet switched on, and he heard the voice of Aaron Kurtzman. He stared at the trees as he listened. Fire danced along the trunk and branches of one large pine, but the blaze didn't seem out of control. Kissinger saw no sign of the wreckage itself or evidence of survivors.

"John, our radar scan picked up three small blips from the chopper before it went down," Kurtzman announced. "They came down slowly and touched ground by a clearing about two hundred yards in diameter."

"You mean they bailed out?" Kissinger asked with surprise.

"Looks that way. They used the treetops for cover and jumped. It took a lot of guts to parachute from less than one hundred yards from the ground, but we're talking about Able Team.''

"Yeah. Lyons would have done it without a chute if he had to. He could probably dive into the trees and grab a branch like Tarzan.''

"They might have some broken bones, but I wouldn't count on them being out of action.''

"If we can get there fast enough, we might be able to get them before they can ditch their chute harnesses and prepare any type of ambush.''

"I wouldn't count on that, either.''

The caravan of Jeeps continued toward the crash site, with Kissinger's vehicle in the lead. He gripped the stun gun in one fist, finger near the trigger. The armorer had managed to load the special antiriot motor on the Jeep before they charged to the trees, but it would be useless if he had to use it in an area with thick brush and low tree branches.

He saw the rotor blades and part of the chopper's mangled fuselage among the flames. Debris scattered across the ground, and the blaze roared as it consumed spilled fuel. The tank had already blown, and there was no risk of another explosion from the ruins. Kissinger glanced around the area and spotted a clump of white silk jammed along the fork of a tree branch. An empty harness dangled from long cords. Apparently, someone had shed the parachute in a hurry and allowed an updraft to carry it into the tree. No time had been wasted to hide the silk.

"They're around here somewhere. Stop the Jeep. We have to find them.''

Kissinger scanned the familiar woodlands with new apprehension. Bushes and tree trunks suddenly appeared to be ideal cover for a deadly ambush. A good warrior knew how to make the most of natural camouflage, and Able Team was good. Kissinger recalled Gadgets Schwarz was particularly good at silent killing techniques, and Blancanales excelled in camouflage.

The other vehicles rolled closer and reduced speed when the drivers saw that Kissinger's rig had stopped. The last Jeep crept forward, the driver's attention fixed on the vehicles and the wreckage. He failed to notice the lean shape rise from some tall grass near his rig.

Gadgets Schwarz suddenly bolted alongside the Jeep, yanked open the door with one hand while the other chopped the driver across the wrists, forcing him to release the steering wheel. Before the startled man could react, Schwarz swept a forearm across his helmeted head to shove the man sideways. A slight pull was all he needed to send the driver in an awkward tumble from the Jeep.

The blacksuit in the passenger seat didn't have an opportunity to stop Schwarz. Carl Lyons had appeared from behind a tree trunk an instant after Schwarz made his move. He hit the rig from the passenger side, wrapping one muscled arm around the second man's head while his other fist sank into the passenger's lap. Knuckles struck hard. A protective cup spared the man from a blow that might have castrated him, yet the force and unexpected impact left him dazed and wheezing in pain.

Lyons gripped the man by the belt, used it as a handle and heaved him from the seat. He lifted the stunned figure over the door without having to open it and tossed him aside. Lyons hopped into the seat while Schwarz got behind the wheel and put the Jeep in reverse.

"Hey!" a member of the defense team in the next vehicle exclaimed. "What the fu—"

Lyons swung his arm around the edge of the windshield, his big Colt Python in his fist. A guy riding shotgun in the second vehicle started to rise, a Taser stun gun in his fist. Lyons triggered his revolver before the man could aim his weapon. A .357 Magnum slug slammed into the security man's chest. The powerful round sent him over the rim of the Jeep door and crashing to the ground, flak vest dented by the projectile.

The gunshot alerted the others to the situation. Attention turned to the Jeep confiscated by the Able Team commandos. It was heading for the main house while Kissinger's group tried to turn their vehicles to give chase. The driver of the Jeep, who had seen his passenger get shot out of the rig, hit the gas, spinning his wheels in an effort to rush for cover. But he had managed only to pull his vehicle into the path of another Jeep, further hampering their progress. The rig came to an abrupt halt, almost broadsided by the nose of the advancing Jeep.

"What are you doing, you idiot!" a voice demanded.

"Did you see what happened?" the rattled driver replied as he turned the steering wheel with shaky hands.

He started to move past some bushes and a small pine tree. A long branch seemed to slide up from the bush by his door. Suddenly, it slammed into his helmet, forcing his visor into the steering wheel.

Rosario Blancanales emerged from the bushes, both hands on the shaft of his maple cane. He held the crook of the cane under the man's trapped arm and pinned his shoulder as he turned to brace his back and the butt of the cane against the frame of the Jeep. This allowed him enough leverage to haul the hapless driver from the seat and propel him over the top of the door.

"Dammit!" a voice exclaimed.

The man swung a short-barreled weapon toward Blancanales. He ducked beside the Jeep a split second before a bean-bag-style projectile struck the edge. It burst open, spilling its shot harmlessly on the ground. The guy, without wasting time trying to reload the stun gun, jumped from the rig and drew a rubber baton from a belt ring. The driver of the blocked vehicle also decided that was the best move and climbed out to join his partner.

The pair approached Blancanales. The Able Team commando held his cane in one hand and moved the other toward a 9 mm pistol under his arm. The blacksuit hesitated, aware that no body armor was truly bulletproof. However, Blancanales didn't draw his handgun.

"Okay!" he announced. "We do it with sticks. *¡Muy bien!*"

Blancanales gripped the cane with both hands, held low in a relaxed *bo jitsu* stance. The blacksuits knew their best chance was to attack in unison. Trying to handle two opponents would clearly be more difficult than one at a time. They charged, batons held ready. However, Blancanales swiftly moved to the left with a long stride that carried him beyond the reach of the first blacksuit. His cane swung into the rib cage of the other man before the guy could use his shorter club.

Despite the body armor, the blow sent the man staggering into the path of the other blacksuit. Their bulky protective gear didn't help them with agility. They slammed together with a mutual groan.

Blancanales swiftly struck with his cane, chopping his opponent across a wrist and fist. The baton fell from the man's numbed hand as Blancanales quickly thrust his *bo* stave into the visor of the second opponent. The end of the cane hit hard, but the tough plastic held fast. Nonetheless, the blow shoved the helmet back, sliding it from the blacksuit's head. The whiplash effect sent him backward several steps.

Although no longer armed with a rubber club, the first man rushed Blancanales, both hands aimed for the cane. If he could prevent the commando from using the *bo* stick, he figured they'd be able to subdue Blancanales. The Able Team commando met the man's charge and raised his cane. The shaft between his fists served as a solid bar as he slammed it into the blacksuit's forearms, blocking his attack.

The solid maple pole swung high as Blancanales suddenly stepped to the left of his befuddled adversary. He dropped to one knee and performed a sudden low sweep with the cane. Wood caught the man across the calves. His feet left the ground and the man was on his back, dazed and winded by the unexpected fall.

Blancanales started to rise as the other blacksuit attacked, rubber baton held high. The Able Team commando saw motion out of the corner of his eye and swung his cane to meet his opponent's riot club. Wood met rubber. The motion of Blancanales's body added force to his stroke as he got to his feet and advanced. His left hand reached out to grasp the other man's wrist before the guy could use the club again.

The Able Team commando altered his grip on the cane and thrust one end behind the blacksuit's hip and the other against the biceps of the man's extended arm. Blancanales still held the wrist with his other hand as he stepped forward and pushed with the cane. Pressure on the arm and hip broke his adversary's balance as the Able Team warrior suddenly knelt once more. The man went down to the ground with him, his arm pinned under the cane.

Without a helmet, his face and head were vulnerable. Frightened eyes looked at Blancanales, aware his fate rested in the actions the commando would choose at that moment. Blancanales whipped a backfist across the fallen man's jaw, then slammed the bottom of his fist into the bridge of the man's nose. The blacksuit uttered a moan that seemed to express relief even as he lost consciousness.

Kissinger and the last remaining member of his defense team ran toward Blancanales. The Stony Man weapons expert carried the motor under one arm and his stun gun in the other fist. Kissinger wasn't sure what shape his security force was in. Most of them were down, and he hoped none was seriously injured. At least Blancanales had decided to use his cane instead of a gun. Kissinger still had no intentions of getting close enough to take him in hand-to-hand combat. Not as long as the *bo-jitsu*-trained commando had that solid maple cane.

He thrust the muzzle of his stun gun between some bush twigs and aimed at the Able Team pro. Blancanales saw the weapon and dived for the ground just as Kissinger squeezed the trigger. A bean-bag projectile sailed past the prone figure. Kissinger's companion broke cover to point his stun gun at Blancanales. The commando had already drawn his pistol and opened fire before the blacksuit could try to take him down. The armorer heard a 9 mm round strike the man's flak vest and saw his man hit the dirt hard.

He was next, Kissinger realized as he knelt by the bush and canted the stocky barrel of the motor. He judged distance as best he could, aware Blancanales had aimed his pistol at the armorer's position. He fired the motor and felt something strike his protective vest. The crack of a high-velocity projectile breaking the sound barrier confirmed he had been hit by another Parabellum round. A hammerlike blow knocked him sideways, and the sharp pain under his left lung seemed to shut down his power to breathe.

Kissinger lay on the ground, stunned, but clearly conscious. He peered between leaves to see the stun gun had ejected its payload above Blancanales. The capsule burst, releasing a wire-mesh net. It descended upon the startled commando before he could avoid it. Batteries, set in the weighted corners of the net, transmitted a powerful electrical charge as the netting made contact with Blancanales. Kissinger watched the Able Team member convulse from the high-voltage shock, then collapse within the net.

Kissinger took a deep breath. His side ached, but the pain became dull rather than sharp. It might be a cracked rib, he guessed, or maybe only bruised. He started to rise, clenching his teeth in response to his protesting body. A voice called to him from the helmet radio.

"John?" Kurtzman shouted. "John, can you hear me?"

"Yeah," he muttered. "Stop, yelling. I hear you."

"What's wrong? Your voice sounds strained."

"I'll live. Carl and Gadgets are headed your way. We were lucky to stop Rosario."

"They got through all your guys?"

"There are still four by the main house, but I wouldn't count on them stopping those two. I'm going to try to get there after I secure Pol. I sure don't want him to get up and start kicking ass again.''

"Better put at least two sets of cuffs on him and check for any keys, hacksaw blades and stuff like that. Able Team knows all those escape tricks.''

"Yeah. I have to worry about him trying to commit suicide too. It's hard to imagine a nice Catholic boy like Blancanales doing that, but I can't take any chances. I'll try to get some of my guys ready, too. I don't think some of them are going to be able to take on any tough characters for the next few days. A couple of them might be hurt pretty bad.''

"Will somebody have to contact their families with the bad news?''

"I'm not sure yet, Bear. God, I hope not.''

"Well, I'm not about to roll out of my computer cave here and try to challenge them to arm wrestle,'' Kurtzman said. "Guess we'll try to sit tight and hope you can take care of this.''

"Since your people are the high-tech big thinkers, maybe you can keep them from getting inside the house or ambush them somehow when and if they do.''

"We'll try to come up with something. Striker and Jack have appeared on radar, and they should be over the Farm any minute. I'll contact them by radio and let them know what to expect.''

"If they got Kevlar they'd better put it on. Able Team is shooting live ammo and they don't recognize us as friends. They're not pulling any punches, either. Whatever happened to them, it hasn't affected their reflexes, skill or cunning.''

"I'm not sure if that's good news or bad.''

The sound of chopper blades drew Kissinger's attention. A Bell chopper, no doubt piloted by Grimaldi with the Executioner as the sole passenger.

"Hurry up, Striker," he remarked, more to himself than Kurtzman. "We need you now."

MACK BOLAN GAZED DOWN at Stony Man Farm from the copilot's seat. Fire still raged at the south section, and three Jeeps were positioned near the burning wreckage. A fourth Jeep was headed straight for the main house. Even from the air, Bolan recognized the blond head and hulking physique of Carl Lyons in the vehicle and Gadgets Schwarz behind the wheel.

Two blacksuits, clad in riot gear and helmets, boldly tried to cut off the Jeep. Astride motorcycles, they rode forward to meet the vehicle. One hurled a grenade at the Jeep, which exploded behind the racing rig, spewing a thick column of green smoke. Probably tear gas, Bolan guessed. It might have worked in an enclosed area but not outdoors with the wind.

The other cyclist aimed a pistol at the Jeep and seemed to fire a couple shots at the front tire. It was unlikely that would work either, the Executioner thought. Reinforced rubber wouldn't puncture easily, and a couple leaks wouldn't flatten a tire fast enough to stop determined opponents. Besides, trying to hit a moving target was almost impossible.

The tactic didn't work. Lyons responded with his .357 pistol and didn't attempt to disable the motorcycles. He fired directly at the riders. Deadly accurate with the Python, the Able Team leader took one guy out of the saddle with a direct hit to the torso. The second man wasn't stopped by a bullet. Instead he lost control of his bike and crashed in a wild cartwheel tumble.

"Holy shit!" Grimaldi exclaimed. "Able Team is really taking on home base!"

"Looks like they're winning, too," Bolan remarked grimly.

Two more blacksuits set up thick steel shields for cover and made a stand against the men in the Jeep. Apparently, they gave up trying to handle Able Team with nonlethal tactics and fired subguns from their shelter. Schwarz steered the rig in a fast zigzag pattern to present a more difficult target. The Jeep closed in fast and slammed into one shield, knocking the man at least four yards. The second guy broke cover and tried to run, only to be brought down by another .357 Magnum round fired by Lyons.

"I don't believe this," Grimaldi said. "They're killing our own people down there!"

The Jeep pulled up to the front of the main house. Lyons and Schwarz jumped from the rig and raced to the door. An access code was needed to get inside, but Able Team knew it and the variation number used when the place faced a crisis situation. The door opened, and the commandos entered.

"We have to get down there and stop them," Bolan said in a solemn tone that sounded more calm than how he actually felt.

"God, Sarge," the pilot stated. "You don't think we'll have to kill them...."

"I said stop them," the Executioner replied, "and I mean any way that's necessary, Jack."

11

"Damn!" Akira Tokaido exclaimed as he punched a keyboard by his terminal, eyes fixed on the screen. "They got through the front door. Man, I should have got into the program faster. Those guys move fast."

Huntington Wethers looked at the columns of numbers on the screen. Numerals changed rapidly. A program title declared Tokaido had gotten on-line with the mainframe and the code series numbers. Wethers frowned.

"What are you doing?" he asked. "Changing the access codes?"

"Damn right," Tokaido confirmed. "Set the numbers to alter by multiplication. Each number is multiplied by the next number and rounded out to the closest whole number according to the binary language of the system. Nine times seven is sixty-three, so that gets chopped down to six or two-two and two. The last number is decided by taking the combined total of the others, divided by the number of separate numerals, which is seven, and the sum is rounded off like the others."

"Cute," Wethers said with little enthusiasm. "You think that will keep Able Team out?"

"It'll take them a while to determine what the new number is, since it isn't one of our standard codes. If they can't get through the access codes to the Computer Room or the War Room, they can't really sabotage the Farm or get inside and kill everybody. The latter is of a personal interest to me as I'm sure it is to you, because we're among those who could get killed.''

Aaron Kurtzman rolled through the aisle in his chair. He neither praised nor criticized Tokaido's strategy. Maybe it would work and maybe it wouldn't. He pulled open a drawer and searched the contents, muttering with disgust, then moving to another.

"Looking for something special?" Wethers asked.

"Something that could be used as a weapon, just in case. Something better than a ballpoint pen or the tray to a word processor. I should have gotten my gun out of my room.''

"Look," Wethers said, "it'll take them a while to get through these steel doors. They'll probably try to use explosives when the code doesn't work. That means they'll have to break into the arms room or improvise something from the supplies in storage.''

"Right," Tokaido agreed. "Mack and Jack have just landed outside. Cowboy will join them soon with some of his men, and together they should be able to take Carl and Gadgets.''

"Yeah?" Kurtzman replied, unconvinced. "Well, how long is the cord to that copying machine?''

He pointed at the machine in question. Wethers moved behind it and reached down, unplugging the copier. He held up the cord as if examining a captured rattlesnake.

"A little less than a yard long," he announced.

"It'll have to do," Kurtzman said as he took a small pocketknife from his shirt. "Cut that sucker off near the base, Hunt. It's sort of hard for me to get to it.''

Wethers obliged. He handed the cut cord and knife to Kurtzman. He nodded his thanks and began to strip plastic from the wires at the cut end. Tokaido watched him with surprise.

"What are you doing?" he asked.

"Making something I hope we won't have to use," Kurtzman answered. "Plug this in, and the exposed wires will deliver a pretty nasty shock. It might not be enough to really disable an opponent, but the charge will be increased dramatically with a conductive substance on the floor. Like water."

"Geez," Wethers said, "do you know that might be lethal?"

"So might a 9 mm or a .357 round," Kurtzman replied. "We might not have a choice, Hunt."

"It won't be necessary," Tokaido insisted. "They can't get in here. How long do you think they'll need to break that code variation I programmed?"

"Gadgets is an electronics genius," Kurtzman stated. "He's very good at math."

"I don't think he's that good—"

The computer screen registered an attempt to gain access to the coded door. Numbers appeared on screen and Denied followed. Another series of numbers followed with another refusal. Tokaido gestured at the screen.

"What did I tell you? They could keep trying for hours—"

The steel door slid open. Gadgets Schwarz charged into the computer center, a Beretta pistol in his fist. Tokaido stared at him with astonishment, apparently frozen in place. Kurtzman looked away from the gun in the commando's grasp and scanned the walls for an electrical outlet he could reach from his wheelchair.

Wethers stood quietly behind Schwarz, apparently unnoticed by the Able Team commando. The former professor from Berkeley slowly raised his hands and balled one into a fist. He looked as if he couldn't remember how to make a fist or use it.

"Any of you bastards speak English?" Schwarz asked. "How about Spanish or German? *¿Habla español? Sprechen Sie Deutsch?*"

Kurtzman leaned forward, careful to conceal the cord as best he could. He looked at the expression on Schwarz's lean face. The commando's eyes were wide, muscles tense along his jawline and neck. Schwarz held the Beretta tightly in his fist, too tight for a man accustomed to firearms. Kurtzman saw the pale flesh at the knuckles to confirm this.

"Who do you think we are, Hermann?" he asked.

"I bet you understand this," Schwarz declared and pointed the gun at Tokaido's face.

Wethers stepped forward and swung his fist, chopping Schwarz's wrist above the pistol. The blow jarred the weapon from his grasp. Wethers threw a left hook at the commando's face, but Schwarz bent his knees suddenly and ducked beneath the swing.

The Able Team commando seemed to vanish, and Wethers was startled when his fist slashed only air. A hard elbow stroke to the lower abdomen told him that Schwarz was still there. He gasped from the unexpected blow and started to double over, but Schwarz whipped a backfist to the center of Wethers's face. The cybernetics expert reeled from the blow as Schwarz rose from the floor and delivered another elbow stroke, reinforced by his other palm on top of the fist, which added force to the blow.

Struck in the chest, Wethers was hurled backward

into a wall. Stunned and winded by the punishing blows, he slid to the floor in a seated position.

Tokaido suddenly uttered a karate-style yell and charged. He swung a kick for Schwarz's groin and drew back a fist to follow with a punch if his effort succeeded.

Tokaido was of Japanese descent, but he was no expert in Asian martial arts. He prepared to kick by swinging back his foot in a manner better suited for football or soccer than combat.

Schwarz met the kick with crossed wrists in a classic X-block technique. His hands caught Tokaido's ankle and foot. He twisted and pushed hard. The combination and Tokaido's poor balance on one foot sent the young man backward like a cannonball. He sailed into Kurtzman before the other man could move from his path. The impact tipped over the wheelchair, dumping Kurtzman to the floor.

Tokaido moaned as he slowly started to rise. Kurtzman lay sideways, more indignant than hurt. The wheelchair had tipped near him, one wheel spinning slowly. Schwarz looked at the scene with an expression that suggested he might be confused. Wethers started to rise, a ribbon of blood dripping from the corner of his mouth.

"Gadgets!" Kurtzman called. "You know us! Don't you recognize anything? Don't you know this room?"

Schwarz ignored him and bent to reclaim his Beretta. Wethers lunged from behind the commando, wrapped his arms around Schwarz's waist and pulled him away from the gun. The older man deserved credit for guts, but he was no match for the Able Team commando. Schwarz ducked low, reached between his own legs and grabbed Wethers's ankle. He pulled the captured leg and leaned back. Wethers was thrown off balance and crashed to the floor with Schwarz on top of him.

Tokaido proved he was also no quitter as he launched another charge. Schwarz rose to meet the attack and drove both fists into Tokaido's torso. The double punch sent him backward again. The technician tripped on the wheelchair and took another hard tumble onto the unforgiving floor.

"You guys aren't very good at this," Schwarz remarked as he glanced around the floor for his gun.

He located the pistol and prepared to reach for it. A figure appeared at the doorway. Schwarz turned, glimpsing the new arrival an instant before a boot landed in his abdomen. The kick forced his body upright as Jack Grimaldi stepped closer and thrust a left jab to Schwarz's chin. The pilot hunched his shoulders, aware the other man would probably move into a low monkey kung-fu stance. He guessed correctly and lashed out with his right fist, striking another blow to Schwarz's jaw.

The punch staggered Schwarz. Grimaldi turned his right arm, delivering a side kick to the Able Team member's chest. Schwarz hurled backward into a wall. Grimaldi didn't intend to give him time to recover. He moved in and swung a left hook at his opponent's already battered jaw. Schwarz's hands suddenly rose in an X-block, snaring the pilot's wrist.

Schwarz turned sharply and yanked Grimaldi's arm. The pilot stumbled as Schwarz tried to swing him into the corner of a desk. Grimaldi suddenly raised his boot to the desk to prevent being slammed into it. Schwarz still held his wrist as Grimaldi first braced his foot on the desk, then pushed, sending both men backward, away from the furniture.

Grimaldi hammered a fist against Schwarz's grip on his wrist to break free and swung another kick to his opponent's ribs. Schwarz grunted and weaved from the blow. The pilot attempted a snap kick toward Schwarz's gut, but the commando parried the attack with a forearm to the pilot's leg. Schwarz swiftly moved to Grimaldi's left, body low in the monkey kung-fu style. He hooked a punch just above the pilot's kidney and followed with a kick to the small of the man's back.

Pain lanced Grimaldi's lower body as he stumbled and almost lost his balance. Schwarz appeared beside him and suddenly swung a ram-head punch to Grimaldi's left cheekbone. The two big knuckles hit with greater force than the slender Able Team commando appeared capable of delivering. Grimaldi began to fall and didn't resist. He met the floor with both hands to prevent injury and bent both knees as he glanced over a shoulder, looking for Schwarz.

The Able Team commando prepared to attack from the rear. The pilot braced himself on the floor with his hands and one foot as he unleashed the other leg. It extended to perform a back kick and buried the boot into Schwarz's abdomen. The blow sent Schwarz back two steps and drove the breath from his body.

Grimaldi got to his feet. Schwarz watched him with determined fire in his eyes. The electronics expert took advantage of the couple seconds of lull time in the battle to catch his breath. He didn't seem to be wearing down as much as Grimaldi hoped. The pilot wondered if he would wear out before Schwarz.

A large form slithered toward Schwarz. Aaron Kurtzman crawled across the floor, powered by his thick muscular arms. He silently crept behind the unsuspecting commando, and he grabbed Schwarz's ankles and yanked hard. The commando suddenly plunged belly first onto the floor. Kurtzman seized the chance and pulled himself on top of Schwarz.

He dragged his paralyzed lower body across Schwarz's thighs and buttocks as he grabbed the commando's shoulders with both hands. Kurtzman quickly aimed a fist and drove a single blow to the man's skull, hitting Schwarz behind the ear and immediately rendering him unconscious.

"Nice work, Bear," Grimaldi commented as he approached.

The pilot produced two pairs of handcuffs. Kurtzman rolled aside, allowing Grimaldi to snap the bracelets on the stunned Able Team member. Wethers and Tokaido shuffled forward, bruised and sore, but otherwise uninjured.

"We're glad you showed up, Jack," Wethers declared.

"Yeah," Tokaido agreed, "but it would have been nice if you had gotten here a little sooner."

"Cowboy managed to nail Rosario," Kurtzman said. "That leaves only Carl unaccounted for."

HAL BROGNOLA HAD NO illusions that the steel access door to the War Room would keep out one or more members of Able Team. If they couldn't break the code to gain entry, they would break down or blow up the door, perhaps even knock down a wall instead. The big Fed figured it was best to prepare for trouble than assume the enemy would never reach the War Room.

The enemy? Able Team had been with Stony Man from the beginning. How could the guys become enemies practically overnight? Yet, Brognola couldn't ignore the facts. Kissinger had reported the violent encounter with the trio. Surveillance cameras had documented Lyons's and Schwarz's assault on the house and how they had ruthlessly broken through the defenders outside the building.

Brognola took his position by the conference table, a stun gun in his fist. If possible, he would take down the invaders without the use of deadly force. Realistically, the odds were slim that he could stop one Able Team commando with just an electrical stun gun. If both Lyons and Schwarz charged into the War Room, Brognola knew he couldn't get them both. Reluctantly, he had decided to use the .38 revolver for backup.

Price refused to leave. The gutsy woman stood by the doorway to the bathroom. If Brognola failed to stop the attackers, he would at least draw their attention and gunfire to himself. Hopefully, that would give Price the advantage to strike from her position. She still had the Nova stun gun and also carried a pistol. Which weapon she would use depended on her judgment. The bathroom would provide her with some decent cover and, as a last resort, Price could lock herself in the room. The door wouldn't stop a determined commando in peak condition, but it might keep out a wounded and weakened opponent.

He heard the hum of the electric-powered door. Brognola glanced at Price and solemnly nodded as he gripped the stun gun with both hands. Price nodded in return. The big Fed assumed a kneeling stance, using the table for cover.

The door opened and a shape dived across the threshold. The figure hit the floor in a fast shoulder roll, body low to prevent being an easy target. Brognola had expected no less from an Able Team member. He tracked the motion of the form and aimed the Taser stun gun.

Carl Lyons completed the roll on one knee, his .357 Magnum Colt Python in his right fist. Brognola fired. Twin needles streaked across the room, striking the Able Team captain. Lyons jumped to his feet when the shock hit. His right arm convulsed, needles jammed in the big biceps.

The Magnum revolver hurled from Lyons's grasp. Although his right arm shook out of control, the rest of his body only trembled from the electrical charge. Brognola watched with amazement. The man's physical conditioning and determination seemed almost superhuman. He appeared to be able to keep the full force of the shock from flowing through his arm, keeping the effect on the rest of his body to a minimum.

The stun gun had another set of missiles. Brognola figured he'd better nail Lyons with the second shock wave. He aimed for the commando's chest and stepped closer. The big Fed was unfamiliar with the weapon, and he didn't want to miss with his last pair of electro-charged needles.

Lyons's left hand suddenly grabbed the wires beyond his stricken right arm, and he yanked forcibly. Brognola stumbled forward, pulled by the wires attached to the stun gun in his fist. The big Fed triggered the weapon. Two needles sliced the air just inches from Lyons's left shoulder. The Able Team leader tugged the captive wires again to yank the first two needles from his arm.

Brognola dropped the now-useless Taser stun gun and reached for his holstered .38. Lyons charged. His right arm dangled and twitched, but everything else seemed to work well enough. Brognola's weapon cleared its leather holster as Lyons closed the distance.

Instinct and training dictated he shoot to kill under such circumstances, but Brognola lowered his aim. A bullet to Lyons's knee or thigh could bring down the commando without taking his life.

The hesitation cost Brognola the vital split second. Lyons used the scant time to swing his leg, delivering a karate kick to Brognola's gun hand. The foot-sword stroke chopped the Smith & Wesson revolver from Brognola's numbed fingers.

Lyons's left fist punched at Brognola's face. The big Fed had generally been deskbound for years, but his reflexes had been developed in the field and still served him well. Brognola dodged the attack, the rush of air by his ear evidence that he had barely avoided the other man's fist. The Justice man quickly swung a left hook to Lyons's face. His fist connected with the Able Team leader's right cheekbone, but Lyons's head barely moved from the punch.

Brognola knew he was pitted against a man younger, stronger and in better condition than himself. His only chance to win was to score a knockout fast. The big Fed quickly grabbed Lyons's left arm near the elbow to try keeping it at bay and swung his knee toward the commando's groin. Lyons blocked the kick with his thickly muscled thigh and suddenly thrust his head forward, slamming the front of his skull into Brognola's forehead.

The big Fed's head snapped back, and lights burst painfully before his eyes. His feet left the floor, and he felt a great shove at his right. Brognola sailed off balance and slammed into something softer than the wall. He heard a groan, suspected this might be his own voice, yet realized the sound was feminine. He saw blond hair and a pretty face with a startled expression.

Bad luck seemed to be on a roll. Lyons had managed to shove Brognola directly into the path of Price as she rushed from the bathroom, trying to help subdue the commando. Both of them found themselves on the floor with Lyons towering above them.

"Nice try, General," Lyons growled, "but not good enough."

"General?" Brognola replied with surprise.

Lyons didn't bother to respond as he headed for his fallen .357 Magnum pistol. The man's right arm appeared to be numb, but his left hand could certainly handle a gun. Price raised the Nova stun gun in her hand. Brognola rolled his eyes and shook his head. The idea they could rush Lyons, jam the prongs of the close-quarter nonlethal weapon against the commando's body and take him down seemed like hunting rhino with a BB gun.

However, Price also had a pistol holstered at the small of her back. Brognola slid his hand behind her, trying to locate the weapon. Price didn't move. She obviously realized Brognola's experience made him better suited to use the pistol, although she knew the big Fed didn't want to kill Lyons any more than she did.

"You assholes started this," Lyons commented, but he seemed to be speaking to himself as if he didn't think they would understand him anyway. "We don't have much choice how to deal with it…"

Lyons kept an eye on the couple as he spoke, although he walked to his pistol and prepared to retrieve it. However, a figure in black suddenly charged from the entrance of the War Room and headed for the Able Team captain. Like a panther, the shape leaped onto

Lyons. The force carried both men into the frame of the conference table.

Mack Bolan had arrived. Seeing Lyons reach for the gun, he immediately responded. Taller than Lyons though not as muscular, the Executioner slammed into the other commando and met firm resistance. He quickly bent an elbow and jammed it into the side of Lyons's skull. Bolan then unbent his arm to slide it under his adversary's chin. He wrapped it around Lyons's head, the crook of his elbow under the man's jaw, hand on the back of his head.

The Executioner clasped his other hand to Lyons's head and stepped forward to drop to one knee. The trapped head was pulled with the motion, and the big ex-cop's body had to follow. The burly commando hurled over Bolan's kneeling form and crashed to the floor. Bolan drew back a fist to strike Lyons in a nerve center, but the Able Team leader rolled backward and lashed out with a boot. The kick caught Bolan on the side of the skull.

The Executioner's head rang with pain and he fell sideways. He dropped his hand to the floor to prevent full contact, then pushed himself to his feet. Lyons also rose and squared off with his opponent. The Able Team commando held his left fist at chest level, feet positioned in a *T-dachi* karate stance. His right arm still hung limp at his side.

"His right arm is paralyzed, Mack!" Price shouted.

Lyons raised his left fist in an exaggerated gesture. Bolan guessed it was a feint. He saw Lyons's right leg jerk forward and prepared to block a kick with his forearm, but Lyons's right fist suddenly swung a hard punch to the side of Bolan's face, sending him reeling with surprise and pain.

"Uh, it *was* paralyzed," Price commented lamely.

Fully recovered from the electric shock, Lyons's right arm rose high as he charged Bolan, about to deliver a potentially lethal karate chop to his stunned opponent's neck. Bolan lifted his left arm to block. Brawny forearms met. Bolan's right arm slid along Lyons's triceps and grabbed his wrist. His left hand seized Lyons's forearm as he stepped forward with his left foot and swung his right behind the Able Team leader's ankle.

The combination of the arm lock and the leg sweep sent Lyons to the floor once more. Bolan quickly moved into position to deliver a kick to his fallen opponent's head. Lyons suddenly lashed a powerful arm into Bolan's leg to parry the kick and sprang from the floor like a jack-in-the-box.

Price stepped forward with the Nova in hand, eager to help Bolan. Brognola grabbed her shoulders and restrained her. She glared at him, astonished that he vetoed assistance to the Executioner.

"Don't get into it," Brognola urged. "They're going at each other too fast and hard. They're moving from position to position, up and down, so much you might jam that thing into Striker by accident. Besides, you'd probably catch a punch or a kick if you get too close. Either of them could slug you without meaning to when they're fighting like that."

The Stony Man warriors were indeed locked in fierce hand-to-hand combat. Brognola couldn't help viewing the fight with fascination. Rarely did one witness a battle between two fighting men of such exceptional strength and skill. Lyons might have an advantage of muscle and endurance, but Bolan probably had better technical skills and greater experience. Both had already sustained enough punishment to render an average man senseless. Yet, neither appeared to weaken as they clashed in the War Room.

The pair locked together in a violent embrace. They tore at clothes as they tried to trip each other and deliver knee kicks to hard abdomens. Both men traded short punches. Lyons attempted a head butt, but Bolan jammed a forearm under his chin to block.

Lyons shoved his adversary's arm aside with his palm and rammed his shoulder into the Executioner's chest. Bolan was pushed backward with such force that he landed atop the conference table. Lyons bellowed with rage, apparently angered his opponent had proved so uncooperative. He grabbed the backrest of a chair and swung the furniture overhead, determined to finish off Bolan with a final, ruthless blow.

The chair descended. Bolan quickly rolled along the tabletop to avoid it. Wood crashed on wood. The chair struck the table hard, and Bolan swiftly grabbed it before the big ex-cop could attempt another swing. He lashed out with a leg and slammed a boot into Lyons's face. The kick caught the man on the cheekbone, propelling him to the floor.

Bolan slid from the table and landed on his feet near Lyons. The brawny Able Team leader began to rise from the floor, but the Executioner delivered a snap kick to the man's solar plexus before Lyons could straighten his back. The blow left him gasping.

The Executioner dived across his opponent's wide shoulders. His right hand grabbed Lyons's right arm at the elbow, thumb jammed into the crook. Bolan wrapped his legs around Lyons and locked the ankles to secure the hold. His left hand gripped the man's shirt collar and yanked hard, pulling it tight across the big ex-cop's throat as his forearm pressed into Lyons's carotid artery.

They crashed to the floor. Bolan held on as Lyons struggled to break free. The big Able Team vet bucked and wiggled like a bronco, desperate to shake off Bolan. The Executioner's back pounded the floor, and he nearly lost his grip but he held fast and continued pressure with the judo scarf hold.

Lyons suddenly performed a back roll, landed on his feet and rose erect with Bolan still attached to his arms and neck. Brognola and Price watched with amazement, impressed by Lyons's display of strength and determination. He whirled in a variation of an airplane spin, then turned sharply in an effort to throw off Bolan. The Executioner refused to let go, and Lyons lost his balance.

They crashed onto the tabletop. Bolan grunted from the hard impact and Lyons's weight on his belly and chest, yet he held his grip with bulldog determination as great as that displayed by the Able Team hulk. Lyons's struggles became less fierce as the choke hold and pressure on the carotid cut off oxygen to his brain. Bolan was astonished the guy was still conscious. Most men would be dead if the scarf hold had been held such a long period of time.

Finally, Lyons's body ceased to move. His eyes closed, and he uttered a sound that resembled a soft, yet angry moan. He went limp in Bolan's grasp. The Executioner immediately released the choke hold, afraid he might kill Lyons or cause brain damage. The Able Team leader's chest rose and fell as his body eagerly inhaled and exhaled once more, but it responded by design of nature. Lyons was out cold.

"You always were a stubborn son of a bitch," Bolan told the unconscious man.

He untangled himself from Lyons and gently eased the Able Team commander to the floor. Lyons was once again his friend and fellow Stony Man warrior, not a dangerous enemy about to tear him apart with his bare hands. However, that situation might change when Lyons regained consciousness.

"You okay, Striker?" Brognola asked.

"I don't think anything is broken if that's what you mean," the Executioner replied. "We'd better lock up Carl before he comes to."

"Yeah," the big Fed agreed. "I hope we've got a cell strong enough to hold him. I want the bastards responsible for this, Striker. I want them torn down, stomped into the ground, never to rise again."

"You'll have it," Bolan promised.

12

Robert Yong worked the keyboard to the terminal of a special satellite transceiver. The Kumo Shima Corporation had launched a communications satellite into orbit with the authority of the Japanese government and supported by a network television broadcaster in the United States. The American TV people thought a new market in Japan might save their company. Kumo Shima didn't care whether this happened or not. Their satellite transmitted American TV programs to Japan—which didn't seem to like them any better than viewers in the U.S.A.—and also transmitted a signal designed exclusively by Kumo Shima for privacy.

Major Choi stood beside the desk while Yong operated the computer. The North Korean disliked computers, machines designed to operate as imitation human intelligence without the emotional baggage of love, hate, fear or passion. Yet, those traits made human beings what they were. They were the qualities that allowed a person's mind to be molded and manipulated. Every intelligence operative appreciated that. Propaganda was always used to appeal to emotions, not intellect.

Men like Yong and Kykosawa were proud of their ability to use computers. Yet, Choi believed programming a machine to be a tiny accomplishment compared to programming the human mind. The Kumo Shima virtual reality system would be little more than a high-tech game without Choi's knowledge of behavior modification.

"Lone Star calling Tokyo," Yong spoke into the microphone. "Are you there, Tokyo?"

"I hear you, Robert," a voice replied from the transceiver.

Choi recognized the voice of Morihiro Kykosawa. The Japanese business executive and computer genius spoke English, which was fine with Choi. Kykosawa's Korean was less than fluent and Choi's grasp of Japanese was no better, but both spoke excellent English.

"Mr. Lynch has met an untimely end," Yong stated. "His security chief went insane and killed Lynch before he dived out a window and took his own life."

"I'll have to contact Mr. Henly to express my sympathies and ask if he'll reconsider the trade offer Kumo Shima made to their company. I suspect he'll be interested now."

"Major Choi is here," Yong stated.

"That's right," the Korean announced. "You wish to speak with me, Morihiro?"

"I understand you've decided to use our process on certain individuals without authority from this office," Kykosawa began. "That's careless and reckless, Major."

"You consider this affair to be a type of massive corporate takeover," Choi began. "I think of it as war."

"There's not much difference between the two. But we had agreed to use the VR programs with selective subjects to gradually gain economic influence in the United States. That would weaken the enemy and build up our own financial and ecopolitical power at the same time.''

''Nothing weakens an enemy more than the deaths of their leaders and mass confusion and terror,'' Choi insisted.

''Someone always replaces a slain leader, and sometimes that causes more trouble than before,'' Kykosawa said. ''For that reason, we must choose our targets with care, Major. The Americans might become confused and terror-stricken, but that won't be to our advantage if they respond by investigating every possible trend of violence instead of dismissing it as coincidence.''

''We have the ultimate method of creating perfect assassins who don't even realize what they are. Even if they aren't killed in the commission of their act, they take their own lives and can't reveal any details about programming.''

''Nothing is reliable when dealing with human beings. You should know that better than I, Major. What if an assassin's gun jams and he's taken alive? What if the CIA or FBI traces the background of enough assassins to link them with our Kumo Shima VR training project?''

''Risk is always necessary to accomplish any victory.''

''Reasonable risk for logical victories,'' Kykosawa replied. ''You and your Communist comrades might dream of one day crushing the capitalist West, but North Korea isn't going to conquer America.''

''Not alone, perhaps,'' Choi remarked, ''but the world changes. Asia was once the greatest power on Earth. The Europeans ruled for a few centuries, and now the Americans are dominant. Their power has already started to show signs of strain and fragmentation.

It will dissolve one day, and another world power will take its place. The time might come for Asia to reclaim the crown.''

"I thought you Communists hated monarchs and emperors."

"I refer to a crown in a figurative sense. Besides, there must always be a ruling class. Monarchs rule by bloodline, and capitalists rule by money. We choose our leaders based on their ability and dedication to the Party."

"Politics can be very tiresome when they get bogged down with dogma and arrogance," Kykosawa said with a sigh. "Let us change the subject before we argue about matters that won't be close enough to reality to deserve debate until some time in the future. However, the topic of programming government agents and sending them off to kill their superiors is a concern for us right now in the present."

Choi glared at Yong. The man tried to meet his gaze but discovered the major's hard stare too uncomfortable to hold for more than a few seconds. Yong looked away, aware he had lost the contest of willpower.

"My job is to report anything I consider to be important to our mission," Yong declared. "That includes decisions you make that seem to present risks to us, as well as those actions favorable to our effort."

"You really are American," Choi said with contempt. "I am surprised any Korean features can survive in a man who is so very, very white."

"Robert was doing his job when he told me you insisted upon programming three government agents without discussing the matter with me."

Kykosawa's voice drew Choi's attention to the machine. The microphone was sensitive enough to detect all conversation in the room, and the Japanese was clearly aware of the hostility between Choi and Yong.

"I decided there was no time for that," the major said. "The three men you speak of scored extremely high. Their skills, reflexes and physical conditioning were extraordinary. They were the most impressive specimens we've seen here."

"And you assumed they could cause the most damage to whatever branch of the federal government they worked for?" Kykosawa asked. "What if they had been an elite personal guard to the President of the United States?"

"What loss would another dead president be?" Choi replied. "This barbaric country is only 220-odd years old, yet they have had four presidents slain since America became a nation. Besides, I doubt these men were just bodyguards. One was an electronic genius, another had the mind of a psychologist combined with excellent organizational skills and the third was a born military commander with determination and dedication, a vital part of every character trait."

"So you think they might have been some special unit of the CIA or the FBI?"

"Maybe the military," Choi replied. "A soldier can tell when he encounters another soldier. They had extensive military experience and combat knowledge. Reflexes were exceptional, and all three were in superb physical condition. Especially the big Nordic character. They're all very intelligent. I doubt any of that trio has an IQ lower than 130. All three spoke Spanish fluently and had at least working vocabularies in several other languages. Whatever they're involved with must be very top secret and probably very efficient against enemies of the United States."

"And that is why you programmed them to sabotage their own organization, although you really don't have any idea what that organization might be?" Kykosawa asked, frustration flavoring his tone.

"Of course," the Korean replied. "They were programmed to go into action as soon as they returned to their base. When they see it, they will try to take it out. They will believe it is vital to take out their leader, destroy computers, weapon launch systems and data banks and kill as many opponents as possible. I only regret I couldn't see them do this. Who can guess how much destruction three men of such exceptional ability might cause before they were finally stopped?"

"That's certain to draw attention to our Kumo Shima training program in Texas, Major. We don't need that. It places our entire plan in danger."

"It was too great an opportunity to pass up," Choi insisted. "As a businessman, I thought you would understand the importance of taking advantage of opportunities. A religious person might say this was a gift from God. The Chinese might call it *hau joss,* good luck."

"I'm neither a Christian, Jew, Muslim or Chinese," Kykosawa replied. "Obviously, I don't even follow Buddhism, the religion of my parents. Yet, I believe in karma. You know what that means? It's from Sanskrit and means our actions affect our destiny."

"My actions are meant to help us fulfill a destiny of success and power."

"It's motivated by your personal hatred for Americans and capitalism," the Japanese stated. "That can blur your judgment. As for luck, we make our own by our actions...good or bad."

"Thank you for the lecture, but it hardly matters

now. I assume the deed is done, that trio has returned to their base, carried out their mission and no doubt died in a hail of bullets when their own people finally overpowered them by sheer numbers and firepower.''

"We can still expect some problems from this, Major. Is Robert still there?''

"I'm here, sir,'' Yong replied.

"Will you please allow the major and I to discuss this matter in private? You understand? We just need to talk about some things that are confidential.''

Yong glanced up at Choi and reluctantly rose from his chair.

"I understand, sir,'' he announced.

Yong left the room, Choi moved to the door, peering outside to be certain the man had moved down the corridor before he returned to the transceiver.

"He's gone,'' Choi assured the microphone.

"You've caused us a potential crisis, Major,'' Kykosawa stated, "but your involvement in this plan is vital. Like it or not, you and I need each other.''

"But Yong is expendable,'' Choi said. He wasn't asking a question.

"Too bad,'' Kykosawa commented. "I liked Robert.''

MACK BOLAN SHOVED a final .44 Magnum cartridge into the magazine for his Desert Eagle. He slid it into the ammo pouch of a gun belt lying on the conference table of the War Room. The big Israeli-made pistol was sheathed in a hip holster. A sheathed Ka-bar combat knife was also attached to the belt, along with spare magazines for the Beretta 93-R and an Uzi submachine gun.

The Executioner had already packed a set of black

night-combat camouflage clothing in a duffel bag. Several grenades of different types were included in the gear. Bolan had already donned a Kevlar protective vest beneath his shirt. Of course, his Beretta was in its usual place under his arm. The warrior was ready for war.

Brognola studied the computer screen in the War Room. The Executioner was aware the big Fed had spoken with Aaron Kurtzman, but he concentrated on the preparation of his equipment for the assignment he faced. Life and death, success or failure might depend on how well the slide to a pistol operated, or a bent brass to a cartridge that could cause a weapon to jam.

"Good news, Striker," Brognola declared. "The medical team finished examining the blacksuits hurt during the conflict with Able Team. Some broken bones, plenty of bruises and two whiplash cases, but none of them suffered serious injuries. Good thing they wore body armor and helmets, or we'd probably be planning several funerals."

"That is good news," Bolan agreed. "How is Able Team?"

"Right now the guys are strapped down and sedated. They were stripped and given a cavity search to be sure they hadn't been supplied with any suicide pills or explosive devices set to terminate them if they failed to die in combat or take their own lives the way the previous men had done."

"Autopsies didn't find anything like that with the other guys," Bolan remarked, "but better safe than sorry. What about radio implants trying to track them and find the Stony Man location for another attack?"

"Checked for that too," Brognola assured him. "No surgery scars they didn't have before, and they were x-rayed to be sure. The bad guys aren't likely to do anything like that. After all, as long as everyone thinks security personnel, agents and commandos are just going on crazy killing sprees, no one can prove Kumo Shima is responsible.''

"I have enough proof.''

"Maybe you're rushing this, Striker. Might be a good idea to get some more information about Kumo Shima before you pay them a visit.''

"I'll get information while I'm there.''

"Looks like you're not getting ready for a soft probe," Brognola commented. "Grenades, Uzi, Desert Eagle…that's some serious gear.''

"It'll be a serious visit," Bolan replied.

"We still have a problem getting the Belasko ID cleared after your disappearing act in New York. The Justice Department is trying to figure out what happened, and that FBI guy Grundy is bent out of shape along with the NYPD. I've got Leo making excuses and waving our White House authority, but we could still use another twenty-four hours to get everybody calmed down before you use that ID again.''

"I won't need an ID," Bolan said with a shrug. "Jack can fly me down to Texas. Can he still get a flight plan without the government getting in the way?''

"We can do that," Brognola said. "But I think you're rushing this, Striker. I'm pissed off, too. I want these sons of bitches as much as you do, but you know better than to charge down there like a demented bull. That's a good way to get killed.''

"Hal," Bolan began, "I didn't take the Kumo Shima VR training course. I'm not going berserk. I won't deny I want these people to pay for what they've done, but I also intend to find out how they did it, how widespread their conspiracy is and how many more human time bombs are out there. I also want to stop them from doing this again. The sooner that is done the more lives will be saved."

"Given the scope and potential havoc Kumo Shima could wreak, don't you think this is really the sort of thing we should discuss with the President? He should have all the facts in case this blows up in our faces."

"I'm doing this on my own...or at least the raid itself. Of course, I'd appreciate any help the rest of you can give me. Jack already agreed to transport me to Texas."

"We'll help you, Striker," the big Fed assured him. "You know that. I'm just saying the President deserves to be informed."

"Maybe he does," Bolan said, "but I think we should be sure what Able Team will be like after this business before we share too much information with the President."

"You mean whether they'll still be brainwashed when they wake up?" Brognola asked. "Yeah, I wonder about that, too. They might be insane for the rest of their lives or at least require months or years of psychological therapy. Either way, they'll be finished as operatives for Stony Man."

"Let's not cross them off just yet," Bolan urged. "Able Team didn't behave like mindless killers. Lyons could have killed you and Barbara. Pol showed restraint as well, and Gadgets didn't enter the computer room shooting like a lunatic."

"Lyons looked like he was trying to kill you with his bare hands," Brognola stated.

"He didn't recognize me. None of them seemed to recognize any of us or even understand anyone. It seemed they were seeing and hearing something else. Another reality.''

"Virtual reality," Brognola said with a frown. "Why do you think Able Team kept some degree of rational behavior when the others were just plain nuts?''

"Maybe because the guys had plenty of experience in combat missions and raids on enemy strongholds. Maybe they have stronger character traits or personalities. Maybe both. Let's just see how they pull through this before we say anything about the incident to the President.''

"Fair enough," the big Fed agreed. "We owe them that much. Aaron has some information for you. Blueprints of the Kumo Shima headquarters in Texas, available information about security systems, known personnel located there, that sort of thing.''

"Good," Bolan said. "I'm about ready to go, Hal.''

"Akira wants to go with you.''

"Akira? He's not a field operative. Better he stays with his computers. I like the guy, but I don't want an untrained and inexperienced man on a mission like this. We've tried that before.''

"He's also a computer expert and an electrical whiz," Brognola stated. "Gadgets isn't in any shape to go, and the Bear would have too much trouble moving around in his wheelchair. T. J. Hawkins might be a good choice to go along, but he's with Phoenix Force out of the country on assignment.''

"Okay," Bolan said with a sigh. "Akira can come along, but he follows orders and stays out of the line of fire. Maybe he feels like he lost face when Gadgets kicked his ass along with Hunt, but this isn't the time to prove himself.''

"He'll be fine, Striker. And you might need him. You're not sure what you'll find down there."

"I'm never sure when I go on a mission," the Executioner replied, "but they don't know what's coming for them either."

13

Akira Tokaido stared at the mirror over the sink. He raised his arm overhead, palm open and thumb pointed at his own head. He held his other hand forward, fingers stiff with the tips at chin level. The computer technician narrowed his eyes and bared his teeth in an expression meant to be fierce.

"Think Bruce Lee," he whispered.

Mack Bolan entered the workshop to the hangar and saw Tokaido in front of the mirror. At first, he wasn't sure what the young man was doing, because he appeared to be waving at his own reflection. Then he realized Tokaido was trying to assume a martial-arts stance of some sort. Probably something from a movie, which might have been performed by an actor with no real knowledge of the arts. Whatever Tokaido thought he was doing, Bolan saw he did practically everything wrong.

Tokaido's hands were too high and far apart to parry, block or deliver effective strikes. His feet were too close together for proper balance or quick movement. He didn't position his body sideways to present a more difficult target to an opponent. His chin was raised, throat exposed. Tokaido's fingers were straight and stiff, palm rigid and thumb raised. If he attempted a karate chop, he would be lucky if he didn't break a bone or two.

The Executioner appreciated that Tokaido felt humiliated after being defeated so easily by Gadgets Schwarz. Of course, the Able Team commando was highly skilled and experienced in combat of all forms, and Tokaido had always been a computer terminal jockey. Hardly a fair match.

So Tokaido wanted to get tough. The Executioner didn't need him acting tough. He needed the young man's knowledge and talent as a cybernetics expert. A laptop sat on a workbench near Tokaido. Some sheets of data had been faxed from Stony Man Farm. Tokaido had been busy before he started to fantasize in front of the mirror.

Jack Grimaldi worked on his helicopter outside the hangar. The trip to Texas was longer than the Bell chopper was designed for and care had to be taken to protect the engine from overheating. The pilot inspected other parts of the copter and filled the fuel tank for the rest of the journey. They had landed at an airfield in Georgia and would make at least one more pit stop before they arrived at their destination. The Executioner, a qualified chopper pilot himself, would fly part of the distance to prevent excessive fatigue and strain on Grimaldi.

Tokaido suddenly noticed Bolan's reflection in the mirror. He quickly stroked his long black hair with the raised hand and pretended to be grooming himself. Tokaido turned to face the Executioner. He seemed embarrassed and probably guessed the soldier knew what he had been doing.

"Uh," he said, "Aaron sent me some more information about the personnel at Kumo Shima. Most people think the man in charge of the Texas operation is really the executive who handles public relations."

"Norman Adair?" Bolan asked. "The man Cowboy spoke with at the demonstration in Los Angeles."

"That's the one," Tokaido agreed as he approached the bench and reached for the faxed data. "He's sort of a front man for the company, a white American male who probably makes a Japanese business seem less foreign. Kumo Shima wants to appeal to captains of industry, heads of major corporations and leaders in government. In this country, that means they have to deal mostly with white males, who usually feel more comfortable with people who look and act like themselves."

"If Adair is a figurehead, who really runs the show?"

"In Texas the top guy is Robert Yong. He's a second generation Korean-American, born in California, well-educated in business and computer engineering. He has degrees from two colleges and a tech school. A couple years ago he joined Kumo Shima's U.S branch, and he's been a loyal company man ever since. Apparently, he made a number of trips to Japan to meet with the guy in charge of the whole ball of high-tech wax."

"A Korean-American with a Japanese firm," Bolan mused. "The world keeps changing. When I was first in the Far East, there seemed to be a lot of hostility and distrust between Koreans and Japanese in general. They didn't seem to get along very well and didn't really have much use for each other."

"That's a carryover from the past," Tokaido said with a shrug. "Korea and Japan were bitter enemies for a long time. They fought wars over territory and trade routes. Japan occupied Korea at one time.

"Do you think that has something to do with why Kykosawa hired Yong? He figures he can keep a mixed-blood Korean-American in line easier than a white Yankee devil?"

"I don't know if that's true or not," Bolan replied, "but it might not be useful to us either way. Who is this Kykosawa? Kumo Shima's overall man in charge?"

"Yeah," Tokaido replied, "a real boy genius. He inherited a small fortune from his industrialist daddy and turned it into a two-billion-dollar international enterprise. He's basically a businessman, but he took advanced courses in cybernetics and engineering. Just about everything on the guy spells brilliant. He has established connections with Europe, Australia and other Asian markets, as well as with the U.S. That includes contacts and operations with South Korea, Hong Kong and Singapore."

"Interesting," Bolan commented. "I might look into him later, but right now he's in Japan and our mission is in Texas. How many personnel are at the Lone Star branch?"

"More than three hundred people are on the payroll, but the vast majority are assigned to sales, marketing and distribution. The offices will be closed by the time we arrive. Most employees and execs will probably be gone. The place does have its own security force. They've got almost forty guards, and you can figure they'll have at least ten on duty when we get there."

"Kumo Shima hires rent-a-cops from an agency?"

"They picked their own people, including some with no real experience. Most of them aren't allowed to carry guns or other weapons because it's a violation of their parole."

"They hired ex-cons?" Bolan asked with surprise. "Kumo Shima could probably pick and choose from the best qualified candidates for the job. Why would they want guys with criminal records?"

"Not 'cause they work cheap. Pay for guards there starts at thirty bucks an hour. The average for a security guard is little more than minimum wage. They hired some real nasty hard cases too. No pickpockets or petty thieves work for Kumo Shima security. They've got hard-timers who've done time for assault and armed robbery. Some were convicted for manslaughter. The chief of security and his lieutenants are all military veterans, but their careers aren't exactly pure, either."

"How impure are they?"

"A couple dishonorable discharges for criminal behavior while in uniform. Others managed to get out of the service with general discharges. None of these characters appear to have been success stories since they got out. Most got in trouble with the law. Some seem to have dropped out of society for a while, and a number of them are using fake names and IDs."

"Sounds like they might have been working as mercenaries for a while. But that field is pretty dry these days."

"That's what Aaron thinks, too. One thing is certain—they have some real mean sons of bitches in uniform working at Kumo Shima. There isn't likely to be anyone else in the building, and these characters might treat an intruder pretty nasty if there are no witnesses on hand to see what they're doing."

"I'll keep that in mind," Bolan assured him. "Did you get that information about the electrical wiring in the building?"

"Got that as well as the blueprints," Tokaido replied. "It has twenty-seven rooms that vary in size. The first floor has a couple of larger rooms with a lot of outlets and cable sockets for computers to link to the Internet. It's probably where they have their cybernetics and VR gear set up."

He handed Bolan a copy of the blueprints. The soldier studied the sheets. Plumbing installations clearly identified rooms used as a kitchen and bathrooms—quite a few bathrooms. Most were attached to other rooms, which suggested these were living quarters. Bolan wondered how many guest subjects would be in the building.

"We don't have any information about burglar alarms or other security systems," Tokaido stated. "Kumo Shima might have installed their own."

"A high-tech company wouldn't be without one."

"And they'd probably use their own product line. Kumo Shima produces a number of good quality surveillance camera systems, motion detectors and even heat sensors. I checked out the most likely products, figured they'd use the best and extrapolated a probable setup."

"Cameras inside the building and four or so posted outside?" Bolan asked. "Motion detectors stationed by the fence, maybe at the roof and entrances. More conventional alarms wired to windows and doors. Unlikely heat sensors with so many people already at the building. It wouldn't be easy to determine whether sensors detected an intruder or a guard on patrol. Something like that?"

"Pretty much," Tokaido confirmed with a surprised expression. "You've obviously studied these sort of systems in the past."

"Part of my business," the Executioner replied. "I

doubt they'd use motion detectors inside the building if they have ten security guards on duty. It'd be more trouble than it'd be worth to have signals going off every time a guard passed a detector. Anybody monitoring the system would soon just ignore signals. Camera monitors are a different story.''

''Beating a system like that won't be easy.''

''Everything has its flaws,'' the Executioner stated. ''Are all the Kumo Shima camera spy systems operated by a direct current electricity as shown on your charts?''

''That's how they're designed,'' Tokaido answered, ''but they could be powered by backup generators. That could be used for the whole building.''

''Any evidence they have something like that?''

''No. The circuits and wiring don't suggest it, and we looked into purchases made through the Kumo Shima account at U.S. banks. There's nothing there to suggest they bought generators here.''

''So we only have to take care of the main current.''

''How do we do that without alerting the enemy they're being invaded? If the power goes out, they'll certainly be suspicious.''

''They'll be less suspicious if the blackout includes other buildings, houses and streetlights. Figure you could manage that?''

''You want me to sabotage public electrical lines? That's illegal, Striker.''

''I'm not talking about shutting off power to hospitals. This is tornado country, anyway. Most life-support systems, iron lungs and so forth are hooked to alternate power sources in case a blackout occurs. If there was another way to do this in a hurry with limited information about the site, I'd be glad to take it. A power shutdown in the immediate area isn't very agreeable, but it won't be a real hardship on any innocent people in the locale, either.''

"It would be about three or four o'clock in the morning," Tokaido admitted. "Most people won't even know the power was out until they wake up late for work because their alarm clocks didn't go off.''

"Can you do it?"

"I can knock out electrical power for an area of at least five-square blocks by cutting off a couple cable boxes. I can use a magnesium flare to burn right through them. That'll take out power for at least an hour.''

"I'd better be in and out of there by then," Bolan said. "How reliable is this new electric key gizmo you guys came up with?''

"The EMK," Tokaido replied. "An Electro-Magnetic Key. Actually, Gadgets and T.J. came up with the idea, but I helped build it. The EMK is sort of a skeleton key for electrical locks. Insert the probe, and the computer begins to run numbers in sequence. The electromagnetic scanner reads the numbers in the lock and feels a pull on the ones programmed for the lock. This registers on the computer, and when the entire series of numbers is discovered, the key transmits it to the lock and opens the door.''

"You explained that to me before," Bolan reminded him, "but you didn't say if this thing will work during a blackout.''

"It's battery powered. It'll work and energize the lock with enough power to open it. It'll also work if you place the probe against the metal base of a keyboard lock. The EMK can open almost any electrical door, whether it uses a coded card, a numbered keyboard or a magnetic key."

"Almost any lock?" Bolan asked.

"Well, it won't work if the lock is programmed for a finger- or voiceprint," Tokaido answered.

"Let's hope Kumo Shima isn't that fancy. I'll have a radio to stay in contact with you and Jack. If I need any advice in the field, you might be able to help."

"Too bad I can't go in with you."

"This is really the sort of thing I do better on my own, Akira," the soldier assured him.

"Yeah, I know," Tokaido said with a sigh.

14

The Kumo Shima building stood three stories high, surrounded by a parking lot and a high steel wire fence. Six vehicles occupied the lot, illuminated by four streetlights positioned at each corner of the fence. A uniformed figure strolled the lot and glanced up at the helicopter that passed overhead.

Mack Bolan gazed down at the scene from the window of the chopper. The building was unimaginative and pragmatic in design. Square shaped, with a flat roof, the structure was unimpressive from the soldier's observation point. Of course, a building that didn't attract attention would be in the favor of Kumo Shima's need for privacy.

"Doesn't look too busy down there," Jack Grimaldi remarked, his voice barely heard above the roar of the chopper.

"That's going to change," Bolan replied. "Don't hang around here, Jack. We don't want to make them suspicious."

The helicopter swung a wide arc away from the site. Bolan radioed Tokaido and told him to burn the cable box. Moments later, all lights in and around buildings in the immediate area went out. From their elevated position in the sky, Bolan and Grimaldi saw a cluster of city lights in the distance. Downtown Dallas hadn't been affected by the blackout.

"Akira knows his stuff when it comes to electrical technology," Grimaldi commented. "This is his first act of sabotage. Bet he's ready to pee his pants. Are you about ready?"

"As ready as I'm going to be."

Bolan opened the sliding door as the copter headed back to the Kumo Shima building. Grimaldi switched off the outer lights and used an infrared beam to fly safely in the darkness without being seen. Bolan donned a pair of Starlite goggles that used a special type of optics to increase reflected light. Images appeared clearly in the dark as if dusk had barely begun.

Grimaldi scanned the area with care and slowed the rotor blades as much as possible for the hover, which reduced the noise generated by the helicopter. He spotted the security guard below, but the guy seemed preoccupied with the gate to the fence and didn't look up. The guard ran a flashlight beam along the fence and headed back to the building.

"Don't see anybody now," the pilot announced. "This is probably as good as you can hope for."

"Let's do it," Bolan agreed.

The chopper moved above the roof, roughly ten yards from the surface. Bolan stepped to the edge of the open door. He wore a rappeling harness with carabiners attached. A nylon line was hooked to a bar on the chopper hull, threaded through the rings on the harness. Bolan kicked the loose rope over the edge. It dangled down to the roof as Bolan gripped the line with gloved fists.

He jumped from the chopper. Bolan pulled the line between his legs with one hand and worked the rope above his head with the other. Accustomed to rappeling in this manner, Bolan easily slid down the line to the roof. The helicopter quickly moved away as he shed the harness.

Dressed in black from the camouflage paint on his face to the soles of his combat boots, the Executioner blended with the dark shadows. He packed his pistols, knives, garrotes and grenades. The Uzi remained in the helicopter. It would have been too much to carry for a job that required stealth and mobility indoors. Bolan also had a pouch at the small of his back equipped with the EMK, a medical kit, a roll of duct tape and some other gear.

He moved to the door of a garret. It was locked, but a quick inspection revealed the door to be secured by a latch on the other side. Bolan easily sprung it with the Ka-bar blade. He entered the garret and discovered wires to an alarm system connected to the doorway. Hopefully, the blackout had rendered it useless.

Bolan drew his Beretta 93-R from shoulder leather. A Sonics sound suppressor was attached to the threaded muzzle of the pistol. Thanks to the night-vision goggles, Bolan clearly saw a narrow stairwell that descended to the third-story.

He reached an archway at the foot of the stairs and carefully peered into a wide hall that extended across the entire floor. Doors to several rooms flanked the hallway. Bolan scanned the area, saw no one and ventured forward. A pair of metal doors without handles identified an elevator, but it was probably inoperable during the power failure. No one would be traveling the shaft to the third floor, and Bolan couldn't use it to descend to another level.

The Executioner searched for a stairwell to the next

floor. He recalled the data about the building that revealed bathrooms had been constructed for most of the rooms on the top story. Probably living quarters for guests or permanent parties assigned to the building. Either way, Bolan came for information about the Kumo Shima brainwashing techniques with as little hassle as possible.

A sign above a door read Emergency Fire Exit. Obviously, this was a staircase to the floors below. Bolan headed for the door, which suddenly opened toward him. He reacted quickly and ducked behind the door. A uniformed guard soon emerged from the threshold. The guy held a long steel flashlight and cast the beam in all directions. Bolan remained behind the door and waited.

He noticed the man carried a two-way radio clipped to his belt and a revolver in a hip holster. Ex-con or not, the guard packed heat without any apparent concern for parole violations. The Executioner didn't bemoan the failure of the criminal justice system to keep better tabs on such behavior.

Bolan stepped behind the guard and slammed the butt of the Beretta into the mastoid bone behind the guy's ear. The man uttered a groan and dropped his flashlight, which clattered on the floor as the beam whirled light across the hall. Bolan caught the senseless guard and lowered him to the floor.

Bright light flashed at the doorway, brilliant yellow in the lenses of the Starlite goggles. Bolan turned and glimpsed another flashlight in the fist of a second uniformed figure. The guard hissed a curse as he lashed out with the steel torch for a club. Instinctively, Bolan raised the Beretta, but his opponent was too close.

Metal struck metal, and the 93-R was knocked from the soldier's hand.

The guard swung the flashlight at Bolan's head in a wild backhand sweep. The bright orb slashed inches from Bolan's nose as he weaved away from the attack. He realized his opponent held the flashlight in his left hand and wielded it in a rather awkward manner. The soldier saw the guy move his right hand for the gun on his hip.

Bolan's left hand quickly grabbed his adversary's wrist as the guard drew the revolver. The Executioner's right forearm connected with the guard's left arm before the man could club him with the flashlight. Bolan clawed the fingers of his right hand into the crook of his opponent's elbow to control the left arm while he tried to twist the wrist above the revolver with his other hand.

The guard raised his knee, aiming for Bolan's groin. A protective cup of hard plastic shielded the Executioner from the impact of the blow, but the knee shoved him backward. The guard realized this and pushed to try to gain an advantage. Bolan didn't resist, but moved with the shove.

He folded his left leg and dropped to his buttocks, pulling his opponent, using the man's own momentum against him in a standard principle of judo. His right foot rose to catch the guy at belt level as he rolled backward and straightened his leg. The guard was hurled above Bolan in a classic circle throw.

The man hit the floor hard. Bolan immediately grabbed his opponent's right fist and wrist with both hands to wrench the revolver from his grasp. The gun flew from the guard's fingers, but he lashed out again with the flashlight. Bolan dodged the attack. Steel hammered the floor next to the soldier. Both men rolled and quickly sprang to their feet.

"Tricky bastard!" the guard rasped with an East Texas drawl.

He switched the flashlight to his right hand, probably to employ it as a club with greater effect. That required only a split second, but it was long enough for Bolan to move to his opponent's right and grab the man's arm with one hand. The side of Bolan's other hand chopped into the crook of the guard's elbow to bend the arm.

The Executioner then shoved the captive limb high, striking the guard in the face with his own fist and steel flashlight. Stunned, the man staggered from the blow. Bolan grabbed the flashlight with one hand and gripped the little finger and ring finger of the stubborn fist around the steel tube. He pulled the flashlight and bent the fingers. The man groaned as the bones snapped.

The Executioner pulled the flashlight from the guy's damaged hand and immediately rammed the end into the guard's gut. His adversary doubled over, gasping, and Bolan whipped the steel cylinder across the side of his jaw. Once more, the guard hit the floor, but this time he wouldn't get up for a while.

Bolan took the duct tape from his pouch and bound the unconscious guards. He wrapped several layers around their wrists and ankles to secure them before he taped their mouths. Frisking the pair, he relieved them of knives, keys and other items that might have been used to cut themselves free. He removed the batteries from their two-way radios and the .38-caliber shells from their revolvers before dumping everything into a trash can.

Time wasn't in his favor. He returned to the stairwell, Beretta pistol held ready, and began descending to the next level. Bolan found another door at the foot of the stairs. He opened it slowly and peered at the second-story hallway, alert to the possibility that more guards patroled the building.

He saw no one as he emerged from the stairwell. The soldier scanned the rows of doors and hoped he would recognize what he sought when—and if—he found it. He passed two small, narrow wooden doors with standard knobs. Probably closets for office or cleaning supplies, he guessed.

Bolan found a metal door with a numbered keypad access panel mounted on the frame. The panel had to have a backup battery. He reached into the pouch for the EMK. It was time to see how well Stony Man's newest gizmo worked in the field. The device resembled a hobbyist glue gun with a thick plastic handle, molded for finger grips. The probe extended when the trigger was pulled. Bolan placed it by the panel. A digital window on the handle displayed a blur of numbers and selected the numeral five. It repeated this process to choose the next number and so on.

The Executioner heard footsteps. Shoe leather on a hard surface, muffled by a barrier, suggested someone in the stairwell behind a door. He kept the Electro-Magnetic Key on the panel as it continued to decode the access numbers while Bolan searched for the stairs' entrance. Another door labeled Emergency Fire Exit told him where the newcomers would arrive.

The metal door slid open in response to the EMK. Success was burdened by the stress of more opponents about to appear on the scene. Bolan reminded himself he wore the Starlite goggles and whoever stepped into the dark hallway wouldn't see as well as he did. The door to the room stood open, certain to be noticed by any search of the hallway with a flashlight beam.

However, Bolan was a black shape among other shadows, clad in his night camouflage. If that shape wasn't obviously that of a man, the enemy might fail to notice him. Bolan quickly moved to the wall opposite the open door and dropped to the floor. He sprawled to full length, arms extended, elbows bent and both hands around the Beretta in a firm combat grip.

Two figures entered through the stairway door. Flashlights swung in their grasps. One man held a two-way radio, and the other guard had a hand on the holster at his hip, ready to draw the revolver like a Western gunslinger.

"Don't see Jim or Corey," the guy with the radio announced. "They must be on the top floor."

"They were goin' up to check the roof," a voice replied from the radio, barely detectable above static. "Shouldn't have taken 'em this long."

"Oh, shit!" the guard exclaimed.

He trained his flashlight on the open doorway. Both guards approached while the one with the radio reported they had found a "goddamn door standin' open." Bolan remained in the prone stance, pistol held ready in case the pair discovered him. However, no flashlight beams moved toward his position.

The guards reached the doorway. The would-be gunfighter had drawn his revolver and held it in one fist with the flashlight in the other. His partner hastily put away his radio and fumbled for the weapon on his hip. Both had turned their backs to Bolan and didn't detect the soldier.

The Executioner rose and stepped closer. He pointed the Beretta at the pair, but focused on the gunslinger.

The guards hesitated by the threshold to the room, each probably waited for the other to go in first.

"Drop your weapons and raise your hands!" Bolan ordered.

The guy with the revolver in hand turned when he heard Bolan's voice. He didn't drop his weapon, and Bolan responded as the situation demanded. The sound suppressor rasped, and a 9 mm bullet hole bisected the bridge of the guard's nose. The man collapsed without triggering his .38 wheel gun.

"Jesus!" the surviving guard exclaimed.

He dropped his gun and flashlight, eager to raise his hands in surrender. Bolan approached, 93-R trained on the guard. He kicked the revolvers and heard metal skid along the hall floor.

"Listen carefully," the Executioner stated. "Do exactly as I say or you'll wind up on the floor with your friend—and you might not die as quickly. Understand?"

The guard nodded.

"Slowly, unclip the radio from your belt. Key the transmit and contact your control. Don't address him by name and don't say your name or one you make up. If you do, I'll figure you're lying to try to tip the guy that something is wrong. If I get suspicious, I'll pull the trigger."

The guard nodded again.

"You tell him you met Jim and Corey on the stairs. Tell him they said their radios weren't working. They claim the batteries are dead, but you guess they just don't know how to use the radios correctly. Probably messed with the frequency dial and couldn't get it back. Explain that Jim and Corey have headed back upstairs to check the roof. Got it so far?"

"Uh, yeah..." the guy said in an uncertain voice.

"Do what I say and you'll be okay," Bolan assured him. "Get hold of yourself. I don't want stress in your tone. Now, you also tell the control the door you found open was just a supply closet. Tell him you're going to check out the rest of the floor. If you're confused about any of this, ask now because when you start talking on the radio any mistake could be lethal."

"I get you, mister," the guy replied.

"Do it," Bolan instructed.

The guard raised the radio, keyed the transmit button and spoke the story Bolan gave him. The voice from the radio seemed to believe the tale. The guard signed off. Bolan quickly snatched the radio and tossed it to the floor.

"What's in this room?" Bolan asked.

"I don't know," the guard answered. "Never been in here before."

"So we'll find out together. What name do you go by?"

"Ben Hutton."

"Okay, Ben," Bolan began. "What can you tell me? You and the others are ex-cons. Most security companies never would've hired you. Kumo Shima could afford more reliable and trustworthy security. They must have a reason to use you guys."

"Guess they figured we'd keep our mouths shut about stuff they do here."

"What stuff?"

"I'm not sure what they're doin'. They don't tell us much."

"You'd better tell me what you know, or I'll be tempted to improve your memory by putting a bullet in your leg."

"Okay!" Hutton urged. "Take it easy. Some gooks came to us and recruited us. Knew we'd been in the joint, but wanted to hire us anyway. Shit, I didn't want to be a goddamn security guard, but the pay was damn good and my parole officer was pleased that I got the job. Of course, he didn't know they issued me a gun and I was workin' with other cons."

"All of you must have different parole officers. Kumo Shima did their homework. So what do you do besides patrol the halls during blackouts?"

"Mostly hang around the halls at night in case any of the cops here leave their rooms and start pokin' around places the chinks don't want them lookin' into."

The soldier and Hutton had entered a spacious room with shelves and cabinets along the walls. A desk and several chairs stood opposite the doorway. An aluminum air conditioner filled a corner, a thick hose plugged into the wall.

"The cops?" Bolan asked. "You mean the law-enforcement people here for the VR training course?"

"Yeah," Hutton answered. "I don't know what the chinks are doin' with them, but none of us are too fond of the pigs anyway. We kind of hoped we'd find a cop where he wasn't supposed to be so we could hassle him like they used to hassle us."

"You never saw any of them leave the rooms upstairs? Are some of them there now?"

"Sure. They always have a few here. We were told they'd probably sleep pretty sound, but we were supposed to keep an eye peeled just in case."

"Get down on the floor. Lay facedown and put your hands behind your back," Bolan instructed. "Don't try any tricks."

Hutton growled something under his breath but followed orders. He lay on his belly as Bolan knelt beside him and got out the duct tape to bind the guy's wrists and ankles.

"The Asians who gave you your orders," Bolan began. "Do you know for a fact they're Chinese, or are you just using a racist slur as a generic insult?"

"Hell, they all look alike."

"So they might have been Japanese, Korean, Vietnamese, Thai or whatever? Is Robert Yong one of them?"

"Yeah. That's the one who talks like an American. A couple others speak English, but not very well. Sometimes a group of them would come in and tell us they wanted everybody to stay on the first floor. I don't know why. Maybe they met with the cops for some reason."

"They didn't want any witnesses on the second or third floor," Bolan mused.

"You with the FBI or somethin'?" Hutton asked. "Maybe I can be a state witness. You know, I kinda figured these slant-eyed bastards might be enemy agents. Probably Commies from Red China. Those cops are spies too. Right? Plastic surgery was used to make them look like Americans. Maybe they're just on the take. You'd be surprised how many pigs can be bought off—"

The Executioner guessed he had heard all the useful information the ex-con had to offer. He wrapped some tape across the guy's mouth and warned him to stay on his belly. Bolan knew the rest of the guard force would soon wonder why none of the four sentries had remained in radio contact, and someone would come to investigate. Time was running out, and he had to wrap up business at the Kumo Shima building as fast as possible.

The soldier checked the desk first. He jimmied a drawer lock with the blade of his Ka-bar combat knife and found a few notes written in English and in Asian ideographic characters. The style employed numerous small ovals and block-shape lines. Bolan thought it was Korean, but he couldn't read the language. He gathered up the notes and stuffed them into his pouch.

The cabinets proved a disappointment. Bolan opened them to find office supplies, and computer manuals written in English, Korean and another Asian ideographic language he guessed to be Japanese.

The most unusual item Bolan found in the cabinets was a large canister labeled as thioridazine. He wasn't quite sure what the chemical compound was used for, but suspected it to be a type of tranquilizer. Bolan used a small camera with a night lens to photograph the canister and snapped a few more shots of the room.

While taking the pictures, Bolan noticed a framed painting of a rodeo cowboy astride a bucking bronco. It caught his attention because it seemed out of place with the almost sterile setting of the office. The rodeo scene certainly didn't reflect the tastes of the Asian or Asian-American who used the room.

He examined the painting and ran a gloved finger along the frame, discovering a hidden latch on the side. The soldier pressed it and the painting swung open, revealing a wall safe. The combination was programmed by another number panel. Bolan used the EMK and swiftly broke the code to allow access.

The door to the safe opened. The soldier peered inside and found it empty. He reached in and felt for any hidden compartments. There was none. Disappointed, he closed the safe and headed for the door. Bolan pressed the button to the transceiver unit in his shirt pocket. A throat microphone and earplug allowed him to communicate with Grimaldi.

"Falcon," he said quietly, "you read me?"

"Read you, Sarge," Grimaldi replied. "Picked up our computer friend. You need his advice for anything? I can put him on."

"I'm running out of time and need to get out of here."

"We're on our way."

Bolan left the room, hurrying through the hall toward the stairwell. Footsteps warned more guards approached from the first level. The Executioner reached the third story, but heard voices exclaim from the stairwell, revealing the guards had discovered the corpse of the guy he had shot on the second level.

The Executioner continued through the hall. He glanced at the figures of the two men he had previously encountered. They had regained consciousness, but remained helpless and bound by the duct tape. The pair squirmed, wrists and ankles still secured and mouths silenced by tape.

Bolan headed for the stairs to the roof. A flashlight beam streaked into the hall as a member of the guard search party entered the top level. The Executioner whirled, dropped to one knee and swung his Beretta toward the white orb held by the uniformed guard, seeing the outline of the man's head, shoulders and upper body. Bolan triggered two shots. The silenced pistol coughed Parabellum destruction, and the target convulsed from the impact.

He saw his adversary hit the floor and jumped to his feet, continuing to move toward the final flight of stairs.

Another flashlight appeared at the end of the hall. Bolan switched the 93-R selector to the 3-round-burst mode. He blasted a trio of rapid-fire 9 mm rounds at the enemy, intending to discourage pursuit rather than to take down a target.

Bolan recalled Hutton's claim police officers and federal agents stayed in rooms on this floor. He didn't want to rouse them from slumber to join the crooked guard force. The burst bought him a few seconds, and Bolan used them to race for the stairs to the roof. Angry voices announced the enemy had spotted him and were still coming.

Bolan extended his arm, pointing the Beretta behind him at the foot of the stairs as he rushed to the garret above. Two uniformed shapes appeared at the base of the steps. The guards didn't use their flashlights, aware it might betray their location as they raised their revolvers.

The pair planned to fire blindly up the dark stairs in an effort to take out the Executioner. Bolan's Starlite goggles allowed him to see his opponents in the dim light, and he triggered the 93-R. The silenced weapon coughed a 3-round burst and another gunman collapsed with a lethal dose of 9 mm lead poison. The second guard tried to return fire, but the sound suppressor reduced the muzzle-flash and the noise of the Beretta, making it difficult for the gunman to locate a target.

Bolan had no problem finding the second guard. The Executioner dispatched the guy with a trio of Parabellum rounds, slicing open his opponent's face. The soldier reached the top of the stairs, pushed open the garret door and emerged onto the roof. He scanned the skies with expectation, but neither saw nor heard Grimaldi's helicopter.

The soldier decided to discourage anyone from coming up to the roof. He took a grenade from his harness, pulled the pin and tossed the M-26 blaster down the stairwell and shut the door. The explosion rumbled inside the building as the Executioner jogged across the roof to the edge.

He found no adequate cover on top of the building. The flat roof had drainage pipes installed at each corner, and each pipe extended to the ground. Bolan could use a pipe to half slide down the building if he had to flee the roof before the helicopter arrived.

The soldier wondered how much the guards would risk to come after him. A bunch of ex-cons with a cushy deal as high-priced security—paid to look the other way and possibly strong-arm some cops—might not have much taste for a real gun battle. They might be smarter to clear out and claim they weren't at the Kumo Shima building that night.

Bolan hoped they would be that smart. He also hoped none of the police or Feds would emerge from their rooms and assist the guards, mistakenly thinking the men in uniform were the good guys. The longer he remained at the site, the greater the possibility a member of law enforcement might get killed or injured during the conflict.

The soldier keyed his transceiver and spoke into the throat mike again.

"Where the hell are you, Falcon?" he asked. "It's getting pretty uncomfortable here."

"We're almost there," Grimaldi replied. "Hang on another minute or two, Sarge."

"I don't really have a choice."

Suddenly, the door to the garret swung open. A figure crouched low by the doorway and thrust a pistol across the threshold. Bolan triggered a burst of rounds at the gunner. He deliberately raked the roof in front of the man, unsure if he was another thug or a cop. Bullets struck the surface near the guy, causing him to retreat. The stairs had certainly been damaged by the grenade, and Bolan doubted more than one person would attempt to climb up.

The whirl of rotor blades drew Bolan's attention to the night sky—the Bell chopper. A rope ladder descended from the open door at the side of the craft.

Bolan returned the Beretta to shoulder leather as the copter drew closer and the dangling ladder came within reach. He grabbed a rung and pulled himself onto the ladder. Bolan found a foothold and pushed to grasp the next rung. He climbed higher as the rush of air from the blades above tore at his face and clothes.

He glanced down at the building. A man clad in a guard uniform appeared on the roof, stared up at the chopper and raised a revolver in both hands. The rope ladder and violent sway of the chopper made a draw for the Beretta difficult. Bolan immediately reached for the Desert Eagle on his hip instead.

The gunman fired his .38 pistol, and the bullet sizzled a few inches from the Executioner's weaving form. Bolan swung the big Israeli pistol toward his opponent. The swaying ladder made it almost impossible to aim and fire with real accuracy. The guard triggered his revolver again, and Bolan felt the slug strike his lower torso like a brass-knuckled fist.

The warrior returned fire. The big pistol roared, and flame streaked from the muzzle. A .44 Magnum round smashed into the roof near the feet of the enemy gunman. The guy jumped back, startled and frightened. Bolan squeezed the trigger again. His arm rose with the recoil as he watched as the enemy was pitched backward from the force of the Magnum projectile. His body sprawled on the rooftop and didn't move. Bolan knew he would never get up.

The helicopter swerved away from the building while Bolan continued to climb higher. He glimpsed a blur of treetops and ground below, but concentrated on the chopper above. Bolan holstered the .44 Eagle to better grip the rungs, intent on reaching the safety of the cabin. At last, he reached for the hull of the copter. Akira Tokaido's face appeared in the opening. A hand grasped Bolan's wrist and helped haul him into the aircraft.

"Damn," Tokaido remarked. "That was a close call. I thought that bastard was going to shoot you back there."

"He did," Bolan replied, "but I shot him back."

Tokaido's eyes widened as he scanned the soldier for blood and bullet holes. Bolan's Kevlar vest had spared him from injury, and he showed Tokaido he was all right when he got to his feet and closed the sliding door.

"It doesn't look like you made any new friends," Grimaldi called from the pilot seat. "Find anything worth the trip?"

"Not as much as I wanted," the Executioner admitted. "I just hope it'll be enough."

15

"How much longer are you going to keep us locked up like this?" Carl Lyons asked. "I told you, we're fine now."

The Able Team leader spoke from the steel mesh window bolted to the thick door of his cell. Lyons and the other two Able Team commandos had been placed in storage rooms, converted into holding tanks for the trio. Each cell contained a mattress and a ceiling light with the bulb shielded by a cone of steel rods to prevent it from being unscrewed from the outlet.

"Never thought I'd be treated like a prisoner of war here at Stony Man Farm," Rosario Blancanales commented from the next cell.

"Never thought you guys would launch an attack on us," Hal Brognola replied as he stood in the corridor.

"I guess he's got a point," Gadgets Schwarz admitted, but his tone was less than pleased to make that confession.

Mack Bolan joined Brognola in the hallway. The Able Team members sounded like themselves again, and they obviously recognized Brognola. Lyons turned to look at Bolan.

"Heard you just got back from that Kumo Shima brainwashing factory, Striker. Did you find out how they did this to us?"

"Not exactly," Bolan answered. "I found some notes, but I don't know what they mean. I didn't get a chance to search the whole building. Maybe you can help by telling us what you remember."

"I already told Hal, the Bear and Barb," Lyons began with exasperation. "They've all compared stories with each other, and I'm sure they did the same with what Pol and Gadgets told them."

"Standard procedure," Blancanales commented. "There's been someone posted here to watch us since we woke up in these damn cells. You know we haven't conspired together to come up with the same story."

"Excuse me," Schwarz began, "I need to use the bathroom."

"John will get an escort down here," Brognola said. "Sorry. We have to be careful in case something triggers another bout of illusions and makes you go berserk again."

"Dammit, Hal," Schwarz said, "we're okay."

"You probably are, but we have to be sure. Standard procedure. Well, not really because we've never had a situation quite like this before."

"You guys caused a hell of a stir, and we were lucky no one got killed," Bolan reminded Able Team. "Just be patient until everyone is satisfied the effects of the Kumo Shima conditioning isn't still lurking somewhere in your minds."

"I guess I'd handle this the same way if I was in your place, Hal," Lyons stated. "I just don't like being caged in like this."

"Another twenty-four hours of observation, and we'll let you out," the big Fed promised. "You don't need to repeat your story to Striker. We can fill him in later."

"That's okay," Lyons replied. "I'll tell him what I remember. We were headed for the Farm and suddenly it changed. We knew it had been taken over by enemy agents from North Korea. They had installed nuclear weapons and were going to use them to launch attacks within the United States. They had altered Stony Man's computer systems to carry out the attack. We also believed we were all that remained of Stony Man. The rest of you had been killed, and we'd probably have to give up our lives to stop them."

"All of this just suddenly came to you when you saw the Farm from the sky?" Bolan asked.

"Sounds crazy, but it sure seemed real at the time. We saw the enemy lying in wait for us, so we bailed out of the chopper at low altitude and tried to fight our way past the troops."

"You didn't recognize Cowboy and the blacksuits? You couldn't understand anything they said?"

"Everyone looked Korean," Lyons insisted. "In fact they looked like products of some sort of cloning experiment. Everyone had the same mean expression and emotionless eyes. It was like some nightmare that was really happening."

"Or very sophisticated virtual reality," Bolan commented.

"I couldn't understand anyone because my ears seemed to be filled with noise," Lyons continued. "My head seemed to vibrate with sounds of drums or gongs and howling wind. It was like I had a thunderstorm inside my skull."

"Pretty much what I heard too," Blancanales added. "I remember my head hurt and my heart beat out of control. I thought I was going to die before the enemy could kill me. It even seemed like it would be a relief to get it over with.''

"Yeah," Gadgets confirmed. "All I wanted to do was to sabotage the computer complex to stop the missiles, and then I didn't care if they killed me. I recall breaking the new access code to get inside and finding a bunch of the enemy who looked like duplicates from some sort of sci-fi movie. I wound up fighting a couple of them hand-to-hand. Another guy came in who was damn good. Tough and quick."

"That was Grimaldi," Brognola stated. "Jack said you were pretty tough too. It seemed to be a draw until Aaron crawled over, yanked you off balance and took you out by surprise."

"Under the circumstances," Schwarz replied, "I'm glad he did."

"The crap I saw when I reached the War Room was really freaky," Lyons stated. "I thought I found the commanding officer of the terrorists. Really it was Hal. Barbara looked like a teenaged boy. Then a demon right out of hell jumped me. I reckon that was you, Striker."

"You sure didn't go down easy, Carl," the Executioner said.

"I was trying to kill you."

"No," Bolan replied, "you were trying to kill the demon they planted in your mind. Somehow, they had created a different world inside your head. Sights, sounds and memories came to you that seemed real."

"That's what they did to the others who carried out the assassinations before," Brognola added. "This time we got you guys alive to tell us what happened."

"I'm not sure how it happened," Lyons admitted. "We had used their VR equipment, but it didn't seem sinister. Damn realistic. I don't remember anything that could be called brainwashing."

"What about the dreams?" Blancanales asked. "I remember some weird dreams about being hauled out of bed, helpless and unable to move. The rest seem sort of foggy, but I recall that part."

"Yeah," Schwarz added, "so do I. I didn't mention it before because it seemed kind of silly at the time."

"It doesn't seem silly now," Bolan said. "I found a canister of a tranquilizer called thioridazine at the Kumo Shima base. Akira ran a computer check on it and discovered it's sometimes used to treat schizophrenia. The canister was located by an air conditioner. They must have pumped the drug into your rooms as sort of a mist to sedate you. Then they hauled you down to the VR center, fed you the images they wanted into your subconscious while you were in a drugged state and added a posthypnotic suggestion that would cause the VR world to come to life the moment you saw Stony Man."

"Incredible," Blancanales said. "Why are they doing this?"

"And, who the hell are they?" Schwarz added. "Is the head of Kumo Shima involved in this, or is someone else using the company for a political goal?"

"We're still trying to answer those questions," Brognola explained. "Don't worry. They won't get away with this."

"So put us in the field so we can help," Lyons insisted. "We're not doing any good here."

"You're not doing any harm now, either," Bolan replied. "Just give us enough time to be sure you've fully recovered."

Lyons growled something under his breath and sighed with reluctant acceptance.

BARBARA PRICE GAZED UP at a television news broadcast on the wall screen in the War Room. Police officers carried motionless figures on stretchers, corpses shrouded and strapped in place. Bolan and Brognola entered the room to discover the report on the multiple homicide incident outside Dallas, Texas.

"Your handiwork is a top news story this morning, Striker," Price remarked. "Six dead security guards, two injured and half a dozen law-enforcement officers who are baffled by the incident."

"Did they mention any of the people in the building are federal agents attending the Kumo Shima training course?" Brognola asked.

"Not so far," Price answered, "but the agencies they belong to certainly know."

"That means somebody will tell the President," Brognola said with a sigh. "He's a smart guy and he'll guess there could be a connection with this incident and the bodyguards going on murder sprees. I'm surprised he hasn't called already."

"Earlier on the news they mentioned the President is in a conference with several heads of state, discussing international trade," Price stated. "He'll probably get in touch with you as soon as he can."

"Something else to look forward to," the big Fed muttered. "Has Aaron translated those notes Striker found?"

"Yeah," Price replied. "The notes written in Japanese seem to be a shopping list for computer equipment and office supplies. The notes in Korean are more interesting."

She found the English version of the pages on the table and handed them to Brognola. The big Fed plucked a cigar from his pocket as he read the sheets.

"It seems somebody was spinning some speculation about Carlson, Smith and Ballard," he remarked.

"Who are they?" Bolan asked.

"Cover names Able Team used when they attended that VR training course," Brognola explained. "The notes mention all three displayed high degrees of intelligence, combat skills and experience. Smith's ability with electronics suggests he is expert in computers, advanced high-tech weaponry or both. Even wonders if he might have access to missile silos."

"That's some interesting speculation," Bolan commented.

"It also mentions Ballard could be adept in infiltration, propaganda and manipulation. Carlson could be a unit commander of an elite military outfit and master of strategy. A separate list mentions CIA, the Pentagon and the White House."

"Sounds like possible targets," the Executioner said. "That means they didn't know who Able Team worked for or any details about Stony Man. At least the Farm isn't known to the enemy. They programmed our guys to carry out their raid when they reached their destination. CIA, the Pentagon and the White House are probably just wishful thinking."

"Bastards," Brognola growled, nearly biting through his unlit cigar. "But, how is this random target selection connected to the previous assassinations? The oil executive in Alaska, the robotics company man and the importer-distributor guy in New York don't seem random. They don't seem to have much in common with trying to sabotage the CIA or kill the President. Pliny and Maxwell were congressmen. That's probably political."

"Depends on what you mean by politics," Bolan said. "Pliny was the intended target. His bodyguards were sent to take him out. Maxwell and the cops in D.C. killed during the attack were just in the wrong place at the wrong time. They got in the way, and the programmed gunmen figured they had to go."

"It still doesn't make sense," Brognola insisted. "What the hell is the meaning of the involvement of Koreans with a Japanese company? I thought they didn't get along too well."

"I hate to interrupt," the voice of Aaron Kurtzman announced.

They were surprised to hear the computer expert and glanced about to find Kurtzman's face on the wall screen, ten times larger than life.

"Some information came in from Dallas," he stated. "We got it from a tap on the police computer system, but it'll be public knowledge in a few minutes anyway."

"What is it?" Brognola asked.

"A police report states Robert Yong was found in his car at the enclosed parking lot to his apartment building. He was sprawled across the front seat, dead. He left chunks of brain and blood in the interior of his vehicle. The cops found a gun by the body. They have it listed as an apparent suicide. There was a note found in the guy's jacket pocket."

"Wasn't he the guy in charge of the U.S. branch of Kumo Shima operations?" Price inquired.

"That's right," Kurtzman confirmed. "Norman Adair, the executive vice president of the Dallas operation has already called a press conference. Texas cops agreed to supply him with information because they don't want distorted versions or half-truths to get out to the public. National media was tipped to it by one of those leaks that seem to happen all the time. The conference will be covered live on TV in about ten minutes."

"We'll make some popcorn and get ready to watch it," Brognola stated. "Where's Leo? Still in D.C.?"

"You sent him to New York to help patch up relations with the Feds and the NYPD after Special Agent Belasko took off unexpectedly after Olson wasted Lynch and dived out that window," Kurtzman replied. "That business is pretty much settled now. Striker can use the Belasko cover again if he needs to. I think Leo is waiting for a flight to Virginia."

"Well, get in touch with him and tell him we have a change of plans. I want Leo to catch the next plane to Dallas to look into this apparent suicide and the investigation involved with the incident at Kumo Shima headquarters."

"While you're at it," Bolan added, "you might also access computer mainframes for airports, trains and buses. See if anyone has purchased any tickets on short notice with Kumo Shima credit cards in the last twenty-four hours. Especially anybody who got a flight out of the country with a Japanese or Korean passport. If you don't find anything in the Dallas area, try the whole state of Texas and neighboring states."

"That's a fun way to spend the morning," Kurtzman remarked.

"We haven't even heard the press conference and already you figure Yong didn't kill himself?" Brognola asked the Executioner.

"I think he was sacrificed as a scapegoat because the

real masterminds realized they had sent out too many programmed killers in such a short period of time and the heat was going to be too great for the Kumo Shima outfit in Dallas,'' the soldier replied. "Whoever is behind a scheme like this has to be pretty smart and reckoned it was time to back off, pull out and give the cops and the Feds somebody to blame for this mess.''

"If they're so smart," Brognola stated, "how did they screw up by overplaying their hand in the first place?''

"Hell, I can only guess what happened. It could be too many would-be chiefs involved and they got too ambitious. Both Korean and Japanese appear to be involved. Maybe they had separate interests, pursued them at the same time and slipped up by doing too much, too soon.''

"Or it could just be Yong behind it," Price commented. "The only suspicious notes were written in Korean, not Japanese.''

"Yong was a Korean-American," Bolan replied, "but he had been making trips to Japan, not Korea. You have any data on Yong, Aaron? Does it mention if he was fluent in Korean?''

"I pulled a file on him and accessed information about the guy's background and education. Yong did have ability as a linguist, but, ironically, Korean wasn't among the languages he spoke or read fluently. According to my files, Yong was fluent in French and Italian, and semifluent in Japanese, but he couldn't read it very well. Nothing here to suggest he had any grasp of Korean.''

"It's not very likely he'd make notes in that language," Bolan commented. "Besides, the wall safe I found was empty. I doubt they went to the trouble to install the safe and didn't use it. Somebody had removed whatever was in there before I arrived. Somebody who saw the figurative handwriting on the wall.''

"I didn't think we'd be lucky enough to have the bastard responsible do us a favor by blowing his own brains out," Brognola said with a sigh.

"It's not that easy," the Executioner stated. "It's not over yet."

16

The press conference from Dallas received limited coverage by national media. Most reporters on hand belonged to local or state press. They congregated before a platform as representatives from the police and the mayor explained how Robert Yong's body had been discovered.

The suicide note claimed responsibility for criminal misconduct connected with the series of murderous acts by clients who attended the Kumo Shima training course. Yong's note stated he had supplied steroids to subjects to increase their strength and speed. The drugs supposedly caused a sense of invulnerability and made the subjects feel powerful and confident. Yong's reason was to promote the Kumo Shima program by insuring subjects would give glowing reviews of the experience and increase business for the company.

Yong's note expressed regret for this action because the steroids appeared to have side effects that caused subjects to become paranoid, homicidal and suicidal. Yong claimed full responsibility for this and insisted Kumo Shima wasn't part of his actions. Due to guilt, and certain of discovery and punishment for his misconduct, Yong had decided to take his own life and asked everyone to try to forgive him.

The police explained the incident was still under in-

vestigation, and federal authorities were already involved because Yong's alleged note implied association
with other criminal actions reported across the country.
A reporter asked if that included the murders of Congressmen Maxwell and Pliny by their own bodyguards.
The police refused to comment and claimed they didn't
have enough evidence to discuss any particular incidents beyond the Yong suicide.

Norman Adair, the public relations rep from Kumo
Shima, spoke after the police. He declared the company
was shocked and appalled by the revelations about the
apparent unauthorized and demented actions carried out
by the late Robert Yong. He said the American branch
of Kumo Shima would reluctantly close down operations until the investigation concluded and full damage
control could be carried out to insure such terrible
crimes never occurred again.

Brognola stared at the wall screen in the Stony Man
War Room and growled something under his breath.
The others present didn't hear what he said, but they
could guess. Everyone realized the story was an effort
to cover up the Kumo Shima conspiracy and make
Yong a scapegoat.

"Steroids my ass," Brognola muttered.

"But it's an excuse the public will understand, and
it hands politicians a chance to give speeches about the
evils of drug abuse and promise to get tough on crime,"
Price commented. "Pretty clever."

"And easier for people to believe than an elaborate
program to brainwash subjects with virtual reality technology," Bolan added. "They can even use my raid on
the Kumo Shima building as proof Yong was involved
with illegal steroids. A theory can be conjured up to
suggest a criminal syndicate attacked the place because

Yong owed money for a steroid deal or the hoods wanted to destroy evidence that might expose them."

"That's a pretty far-fetched notion," Brognola said, "but I guess the American people have been expected to believe explanations that are even tougher to swallow."

"When the cops look into the backgrounds of the Kumo Shima security guards and find they're a bunch of ex-convicts, they might guess that had something to do with the raid," Price said. "Hoods killing hoods isn't news. They might think somebody had some old scores to settle with some of the ex-cons at the place."

"They might reckon the ex-con guards even helped Yong get steroids and hooked him up with a nonexistent syndicate," Brognola commented as he chewed the end of his cigar. "If they come up with that theory, you can bet the surviving guards will say they knew nothing about it, but suggest some of their slain comrades might have been involved with that kind of deal. Dead people make good scapegoats."

"That's what the masterminds of the Kumo Shima scheme hope for," Bolan agreed. "They've probably adjusted the computer records for personnel to make sure Yong appears to have personally selected the security guards to reinforce the claim he's the sole villain in this case. They couldn't have known I'd raid the place, but the incident will fit into the whitewash they came up with."

"At least they're going to shut down operations in the United States," Price said. "There won't be any more brainwashed killers coming out of their program for a while."

"For a while," Bolan repeated. "They've had a setback, but that doesn't mean they'll quit."

The images on the wall screen suddenly changed. Norman Adair was replaced by Aaron Kurtzman. The others looked up with expectation, aware the man wouldn't have interrupted the newscast from Texas unless he had discovered something important.

"Glad to see you're all still there," he announced. "Got a couple items of interest from our scan on airport security tapes and the computer records of flights out of the Dallas area. Want to see it now?"

"I can hardly wait," Brognola replied.

"Okay," Kurtzman stated as he consulted a printout. "It turns out several visitors to Dallas suddenly decided to get the first available flight to Tokyo, Japan, last night. Four used Japanese passports and five had passports issued to citizens of South Korea."

"Looks like your suggestion paid off, Striker," Brognola told the Executioner. "You said you have videotapes from airport security. Make any IDs?"

"Yeah," Kurtzman answered. "The Japanese guys were easy because they were traveling with genuine passports, using their real names. They're from the Kumo Shima main office in Tokyo. Background checks proved they're graduates of business schools and advanced computer mechanics and something called the *Tora Shogyo Ryu.*"

"My Japanese is a little rusty, Aaron," Brognola said.

"The Tiger Business School," Kurtzman explained. "Kykosawa started it himself. It seems he wants his top execs to be 'tigers of the business world.' His school includes training in karate and kendo as well as international trade, design engineering of his products, classes on languages and cultures of countries the graduates will do business in."

"Isn't kendo a type of sword fighting?" Price asked.

"Yeah," Bolan replied, "but it isn't uncommon for Japanese businessmen to practice kendo as a form of developing spiritual strength, mental focus and a way to relieve stress. You said the Japanese had genuine passports and used their real names, Bear. Does that mean the Koreans didn't?"

"You can say that again," Kurtzman answered. "They used legitimate South Korean passports, but the names they're issued to belong to infants who died thirty or forty years ago. We haven't been able to identify all of them, but one guy stands out as particularly interesting."

A grainy image on surveillance video appeared on-screen. Passengers were moving through metal detectors at an airport boarding gate. White lines formed around the head and shoulders of a well-built Asian man clad in a gray suit. The lines merged into a square and grew into an enlargement of the passenger's head and hard features.

"This is Choi Sung," Kurtzman explained. "CIA has a file on him. He's a major in the North Korean army with special expertise in intelligence operations, behavior modification and aggressive propaganda."

"A professional brainwasher," Brognola remarked.

"Very professional," Kurtzman confirmed. "He's considered to be one of the best in the field. CIA claims he programmed some human time bombs in 1995 in an effort to assassinate the South Korean president. The would-be killers might have succeeded, but they looked and acted like zombies. Security forces stopped them, and they blew themselves up."

"I'm surprised that didn't make national news," Price commented.

"There was a cover-up because both the U.S. and South Korean intel organizations were afraid it might be part of a larger conspiracy," Kurtzman explained. "Major Choi seemed to have carried out this scheme on his own, and the North Korean government wasn't too thrilled with him. The son of a bitch could have caused a big economic problem for Pyongyang."

"He's lucky they didn't have him executed," Brognola said.

"Maybe they would have if Choi had waited to see what would happen after his court-martial," Kurtzman stated. "Choi appears to have fled the country along with a few of his men. Some of his soldiers were extremely dedicated to Choi. His personality profile and psychological evaluation suggests Choi is a fanatic even by North Korean terms. He has a passionate hatred for anything and everything that isn't hard-core communism."

"And now he's working with the Kumo Shima conspiracy," Bolan commented. "What about the head of the company? Is Kykosawa a Communist?"

"Kykosawa doesn't have any history of political involvement beyond the interests of his company," Kurtzman answered. "You'd think he would be a capitalist, but this wouldn't be the first time individuals with different political views would join forces for a common goal."

"Yeah," the Executioner stated. "Kykosawa wants wealth and influence while Choi wants to strike out at Western democracy in general and the United States in particular. If he's a fanatic, he probably decided to program Able Team to attack us. That was beyond what Kykosawa would have approved of and meant they had to carry out some damage control before they shut down operations in the U.S. for now."

"Okay," Brognola said. "But why would Kykosawa want those previous victims assassinated? Lynch was involved with importing and distributing electronic goods. Maybe getting rid of him made sense if Kykosawa had reason to believe the guy's partner would be more willing to deal with him. But what would be the motive for killing the oil executive or the robotics guy or two U.S. congressmen?"

"We've been working on that, too," Kurtzman declared. "At first there doesn't seem to be a connection between any of the victims, but we did find strong reasons why Kykosawa would want all of them out of the way. Lynch is the most obvious. He hadn't been interested in doing business with Japanese markets ever since major inflation started to hurt Japan's economy. Other markets in Asia offered better deals for his company."

"Didn't I say something like that?" the big Fed asked.

"Not exactly," Kurtzman replied. "Never mind that now. You remember Graham Sutton, the vice president of Watley Oil? He was also one of the biggest stockholders of two of the biggest American computer technology corporations. Sutton had used his influence to lobby against Japanese imports that competed with the products he profited from. He was very good at this because he had a good friend in congress who shared his interests. Especially since Sutton was a major contributor to Robert Pliny's campaign for public office. Pliny was in favor of legislation to limit imports and discourage them by raising import taxes."

"And we already figured Maxwell wasn't intended

as a target," Price commented. "The senior congressman just happened to stop and talk to Pliny when the killers arrived and opened fire."

"So that leaves Brittly, the head of Chapman Robotics," Kurtzman stated. "Of course, we knew Chapman Robotics was one of the leading manufacturers of industrial robots for assembly line duties, as well as those for bomb disposal and military probes. What we didn't appreciate is the designs for those robots were originally created on computers and tested by using virtual reality technology. Chapman Robotics was going to branch into VR training programs with Brittly in charge of design, production and sales."

"He had already established connections with the military and police agencies so Brittly would've been able to sell his VR program more efficiently to the same markets Kykosawa needed to use," Bolan said. "Kykosawa obviously believes in removing any obstacle in a ruthless and permanent manner."

"I wonder what he and Choi will try next?" Brognola remarked.

"They won't get a chance to try again," the Executioner declared. "We know Choi and his comrades have headed back to Japan to join Kykosawa. That means I know where to find them."

"So you're going to Japan," Brognola said with a nod. "We'll make arrangements. I think we can get you a military flight within the next eight hours. Maybe less."

"CIA and NSA have agents in Tokyo," Price added. "Case officers are probably operating at the U.S. Embassy. The Company more than NSA. The National Security Agency is primarily interested in maintaining observation posts in Japan used to monitor SIGINT spy satellites in orbit across Russia, China and North Korea."

"I have another suggestion," Kurtzman spoke from the wall screen. "You might want to take somebody with you who you've worked with before, Striker. Somebody who knows Tokyo, speaks the language and can handle himself in a fight."

"Of course," Brognola said. "John Trent."

"Is he still running that dojo in San Francisco?" Price asked. "I thought he'd be working full-time for the federal government by now. A guy with his talent ought to be in the field more often."

"I don't think Trent wants to work for the government," Bolan stated. "He teaches self-defense and martial arts because that's what he wants to do. He might not be willing to close down his school on short notice so he can run off to Japan on a mission he knows nothing about."

"Are you kidding?" Brognola asked. "Maybe he's basically an instructor, but Trent is still trained as a ninja. He's never turned down a chance to participate with our people in the field. He doesn't even know exact details about Stony Man or your real name, Striker, but he's always agreed to help us in the past."

"Trent has the skill and courage of a warrior," Bolan agreed, "but he's still really a civilian. I just don't like getting civilians involved in a mission."

"He's no ordinary civilian, and he's ideal for this assignment, Striker," Kurtzman insisted. "Besides, there's another reason he can help you this time. Trent knows Kykosawa."

Bolan looked at the face on the wall with surprise.

"Really?" Brognola expressed his surprise. "You sure about this, Bear?"

"Ye of little faith," Kurtzman replied. "Getting information and checking facts for accuracy is what I do best. Kykosawa has made several trips to the United States in the past five years. During his last visit, he and some of his *Tora Shogyo Ryu* pals took part in a martial-arts program that was part of a charity fundraiser for homeless shelters and AIDS research. A number of martial-arts schools in San Francisco also participated, and Trent's dojo was one of them."

"That doesn't mean Trent really knows Kykosawa," Bolan said. "He probably met him, but I doubt the guy shared any important information with Trent."

"It still gives us something to work with," Brognola declared. "I think you ought to take Trent with you if you want to go after these bastards."

"I want them," the Executioner confirmed. "I'm going to pack for the trip. If Trent comes along, that's fine with me. With or without him, I intend to put Kumo Shima out of business for good."

17

John Trent climbed into the C-130 transport plane. He had packed quickly for the journey. His only luggage consisted of a small gym bag and a long canvas case that contained the gear of a ninja warrior.

Mack Bolan closed the door and shook hands with Trent. Despite his Anglo-Saxon name, Trent's dark almond eyes and high cheekbone structure revealed his Amerasian heritage. He was slightly shorter and less muscular than Bolan, but his handshake was firm and his smile sincere.

"Good to see you again, John," the Executioner declared.

"What name are you using this time?" Trent asked.

"I'm Mike Belasko again."

"Good," Trent replied. "I don't need to be any more confused than I already feel."

The plane taxied down the runway to the airstrip seven miles outside San Francisco. Two Navy pilots occupied the cockpit; Bolan and Trent were the only passengers. They buckled their seat harnesses as the plane rose into the sky.

"I packed my sword, a *tanto,* some *shuriken,* a *kusarigusari* and a few other items," Trent said, "but I didn't bring a gun."

"That's okay," Bolan replied. "I brought a pistol

for you. A 9 mm Colt. I know you favor the .45 caliber, but this way the ammo is the same as I use for the Beretta. It'll be easier for us to get more 9 mm refills in Japan, too.''

''It isn't supposed to be easy to get guns or ammo in Japan.''

''You know as well as I that depends on what sources you have there,'' Bolan said. ''The Yakuza doesn't seem to have trouble getting firearms. Isn't your uncle connected with a Yakuza clan?''

''He was,'' Trent admitted. ''He left when he moved to America. For a while he was involved with some black market videotapes and other small criminal deals, but he recently died.''

''I'm sorry to hear that. Was he the last of your immediate family?''

''Yes,'' Trent said with a sigh. ''I hope you didn't think I could help you contact Yakuza in Japan. Any connections I had with them are gone with my uncle's ashes.''

Bolan shook his head. ''No, but you do know a Japanese businessman named Kykosawa who might be more dangerous than any Yakuza boss.''

''Morihiro Kykosawa?'' Trent asked with a frown. ''I met him at a charity function last year. He was polite, but not very friendly and a bit arrogant when he wasn't trying to make points with the newspapers and Japanese-American businessmen who attended the event. What I best remember about Kykosawa was his swordsmanship. He and his friends displayed some good kendo demonstrations.''

''Is he as good with a sword as you are?'' Bolan asked.

The Executioner had witnessed Trent's ability with

a ninja sword in actual combat and knew how skilled and deadly Trent was with the long blade. A sword was an outdated weapon for modern warfare, but it could still kill as efficiently as a gun in close quarters in the hands of a man like Trent.

"I'm not sure," the ninja replied. "I'm trained in *kenjutsu*, not kendo. They're different styles of swordfighting."

"Isn't kendo more a sport form and *kenjutsu* more combative?" Bolan asked. "Sort of like judo compared to jujutsu?"

"Kendo is usually more restricted to limited types of sword strokes one can use with the *shinai*, but I can't really say how well Kykosawa can employ a real sword in genuine combat. He appeared to be better than any of his friends, but they might have held back to allow their leader to shine as the star performer in the demonstrations."

"Try to recall if Kykosawa said anything about his business or if you noticed anything special about him. Did he drink much or show signs of drug abuse? Mention anything about his home, habits, weaknesses?"

"Kykosawa and I only exchanged a few sentences, and frankly neither one of us had much reason to associate with the other," Trent answered. "What's this about, Mike? The phone call I received at the dojo didn't tell me much."

Bolan explained the mission without any details he considered confidential or a threat to the security of Stony Man. Trent didn't appear surprised to learn the assignment was connected to the Kumo Shima incident in Texas.

"The man they say committed suicide was really murdered?"

"Yeah," Bolan answered. "One of our people checked out the autopsy report. Robert Yong supposedly stuck a pistol in his mouth and shot himself, but the end of his tongue was clipped off by the bullet. That means he was probably trying to speak or even tried to push back the gun barrel with his tongue. He wouldn't likely do that if he really killed himself. Also, the bullet exited at his nape, which meant the weapon had been fired when pointed down into his mouth. Most suicides angle the barrel upward to shoot through the roof of the mouth into the brain."

"They want him to take the blame for the killing sprees that have been in the news lately," Trent stated. "Kumo Shima is Kykosawa's company and you believe he and the Korean major are really responsible? What do you want me to do?"

"I had hoped you might know Kykosawa better. However, if he remembers you, it might help us get closer to the man. You speak Japanese, and you've spent a lot of time in the country. It wouldn't seem that strange if you were working as my interpreter, especially if I wanted to meet with Kykosawa about attending another martial-arts charity event."

"I should have packed a suit," Trent remarked.

"We'll get you some more clothes when we arrive at Tokyo. We have to be careful, John. Kykosawa will probably be suspicious of a couple Americans suddenly choosing this time to visit him after what happened in Texas."

"He might refuse to even see us," Trent remarked. "Kykosawa might not even remember me. The fact I'm half Japanese might not be in my favor. I'm considered a gaijin or foreigner as much as any other American visiting Japan."

"I don't think that will be an influence for whether or not Kykosawa agrees to meet with us," Bolan said. "If he doesn't, we'll try some different tactics. Before we can determine any exact strategy, we'll need to speak with a CIA case officer stationed at the embassy in Tokyo."

Trent glanced at a large duffel bag near Bolan's feet. He probably wondered what arsenal the soldier had packed for the occasion. The man he knew as Michael Belasko was remarkably skilled with a variety of weapons, and the bag probably contained a fearsome assortment of lethal hardware.

"You might as well try to get comfortable and relax, John," Bolan suggested. "We've got a long flight ahead of us before we reach Japan."

TOKYO WAS ONE of the largest cities in the world and one of the most modern. The majority of streets and buildings were modern because much of Tokyo had been destroyed during World War II. The new city had been built upon the ashes and rubble of the past.

Mack Bolan glanced out the car window as it crawled along the traffic-clogged streets. Tokyo was even more crowded than New York City.

"You've been to Japan before?" Arnold Foley asked.

Bolan turned to face the CIA case officer. Foley had met Bolan and Trent at the airport. He waved them through customs with an embassy ID and diplomatic immunity. Security eyed their luggage with suspicion, but no one detained them or asked to search their gear. Foley led them outside to the waiting car with a driver, ready to take them to the U.S. Embassy.

"Yeah," Bolan answered, "I've been here a couple times. How long have you been stationed here?"

"Almost five years," Foley replied. "I graduated top of my class in Oriental languages. Japanese, Korean, Vietnamese and Chinese...Wu and Xiang dialects as well as Mandarin and Cantonese."

"That's impressive," Trent remarked. "You must be quite a linguist."

"I didn't mention Portuguese and Russian," Foley said with a shrug. "I had wanted a post in Beijing, but I wound up here. The Company seems to be a little confused ever since the cold war supposedly ended. Instead of concentrating on the Communists, they're busy trying to justify continued operations in places that seem questionable these days."

"Maybe you'll get reassigned after this," Bolan suggested. "What have you been told so far?"

"Not too much," Foley answered. "I know whatever brought you two here is considered urgent, and you have White House authority to pretty much handle this any way you want. I was told to check up on Kykosawa, but I'm not quite sure why. The guy seems to be a businessman, not a political extremist. Something happened with his branch in the United States. I know he shut down operations there on short notice, and there's some sort of investigation going on. Interpol and Kenpei are putting together a special unit to investigate the man here as well. Oh, Kenpei is sort of Japan's secret service."

"I know," Bolan replied. "That's all you've got so far?"

"Well, I pulled a file on Kykosawa and I got the blueprints for the Kumo Shima office building. He also has a penthouse apartment in Tokyo. Luxury pad. The guy's rich, you know. We put wiretaps on his phones at both locations.''

"Kykosawa runs a high-tech computer company," Bolan said. "He won't be discussing any confidential business on the phone."

"We can try to hack into his mainframe," the CIA man said. "It's not my field, but we have some top-notch people who specialize in that sort of thing."

Bolan looked at Foley's face. It seemed soft and pale, the features bland. It was a face that would be ignored in a crowd and easily forgotten. Bolan knew Foley was thirty-four, but he seemed older. His thin lips were drawn taut across his teeth, and he glanced down at the floor frequently. The Fed seemed uncomfortable with Bolan and Trent.

"We should try to make contact with Kykosawa," Trent reminded Bolan. "A simple direct approach."

"You want to call him?" Foley asked.

The CIA officer placed a briefcase on his lap, opened it and removed a mobile cellular phone. He consulted a notepad and then moved a finger over the buttons of the phone. Foley paused before dialing and looked at Bolan for approval. The soldier nodded in a reluctant manner.

"Either of you guys speak Japanese?" he asked as he punched the numbers.

"I do," Trent replied and accepted the phone from Foley.

Bolan's grasp of Japanese was very limited, and he barely understood a word Trent spoke into the phone beyond the traditional greeting of *Moshi, moshi*. Trent listened for a moment and said, *"Domo arigato."*

"I spoke with his secretary," Trent explained. "She

said to hold on and she'll see if Kykosawa will speak with me. She did emphasize he is a very busy man.''

"We'll probably have to try something else," Bolan commented.

Trent's eyes widened with surprise when a voice spoke to him from the cellular phone. He replied to the caller in English.

"Yes, this is John Trent. I'm surprised you remember me, Kykosawa-*san*.... That's very kind of you, sir. I was impressed by your skill as well. In fact that's connected with my reason for the call. Yes, Kykosawa-*san*, it is connected with another martial-arts event for charity. Yes, here in Japan. I'm in Tokyo with a Mr. Belasko. He needed a translator, and he knew I'd met you and hoped you might respond to our offer.... Yes, it is for a worthy cause.... Well, I'll have to check with Mr. Belasko.''

Trent lowered the phone and turned to Bolan. "He said he'll be happy to meet us at the Kumo Shima main office in two hours," Trent explained. "What do you think?''

"Tell him yes.''

"Kykosawa-*san?*" Trent said into the phone. "We'll be glad to meet you, and we appreciate you finding time for us.... Thank you, that's very considerate.... Yes, I'm sure we can find the building.... I look forward to it as well. Goodbye.''

"That was easy," Foley commented as he took the phone from Trent.

"Yeah," Bolan said, "it was. You know where this Kumo Shima building is located, Foley?''

"I'll tell the driver," the CIA man replied. "The bags you brought look heavy. Don't tell me you brought a load of guns.''

"If you don't want me to tell you, I won't."

"This country is tough on restrictions about firearms, Belasko," Foley stated. "Even the cops don't carry guns here."

"I seem to recall the Yakuza have had gun battles between gangs in broad daylight in Tokyo, and the Japanese Red Army didn't seem to have any trouble getting guns in the late sixties."

"That's beside the point," Foley insisted. "If you get caught packing heat, they'll lock you up for life or at least expel you from the country. Kykosawa's company certainly has tight security. Probably metal detectors or X-ray machines. Maybe both."

"I didn't plan to go in shooting," Bolan assured him. "This will be a soft probe. I just want to get inside to look around and see if we can figure out where he might have his secret records and special VR programs tucked away. I'm also looking for a few characters who flew the coop back in Texas."

"You're not going to tell me more than that?" Foley asked with a frown. "I thought we were supposed to be working together on this, Belasko."

"Ever heard of being on a need-to-know level?" Bolan asked. "I don't think you need to know too much right now. If John and I leave these bags with all those nasty weapons with you, will you be able to hold them for us without having a heart attack? You're not going to dump everything in the harbor to avoid trouble with the police, are you?"

"I can put it in a diplomatic pouch," Foley replied. "The police or Kenpei won't be allowed to open it without risk of breaking international law and inciting a major incident with Uncle Sam."

"Okay," Bolan said with a nod. "Just don't lose

anything. Think we have enough time to stop by a clothing store before we see Kykosawa?''

"Clothing store?" Foley asked with a raised eyebrow.

"John and I aren't exactly dressed for the role we're supposed to play," the Executioner explained. "We need to put on a convincing act. Our lives depend on it.''

18

Mack Bolan felt awkward dressed in a suit and tie. The buttoned shirt collar and necktie seemed restrictive around his neck. He chose a loose-fitting, plain black, single-breasted garment.

The fact he was unarmed made the soldier more uncomfortable than the unfamiliar clothing. He gazed up at the Kumo Shima headquarters as he approached, which was larger than the branch building in Texas. Rows of office windows stretched twelve stories high. A lot of rooms, Bolan realized, probably too many to check during a visit as a business promoter. It was unlikely he would be able to find any evidence or even get an idea which room to search.

Yet, he could encounter plenty of Kykosawa's people, including some of his hired thugs or Choi's loyal soldiers. It wasn't a comforting notion, especially when Bolan didn't carry a weapon or even wear a Kevlar vest. John Trent accompanied the Executioner. He wore a black suit, identical to Bolan's attire. Trent didn't appear apprehensive. Perhaps he guessed Kykosawa wasn't the type to order someone killed in his own building, or Trent might have masked his emotions in the inscrutable tradition of his Japanese ancestors.

The pair had decided to take a cab after purchasing

the new clothes at the popular Ginza shopping district rather than arrive at Kumo Shima in Foley's van.

They entered the lobby and approached an information desk, occupied by a woman stationed at a computer terminal and a uniformed security officer who glared at the Americans as if he suspected the pair intended to steal everything of value from the building. Trent stepped to the counter and prepared to address the woman.

"*Konnichi-wa,*" he began. "*Watashi-o—*"

Trent's sentence was cut short. He turned to a trio of men clad in expensive suits and gold jewelry. Bolan's attention also turned to the men as they emerged from another room. He immediately recognized Kykosawa from a photo fax and videotape he studied at Stony Man Farm.

Although he wore a blue-and-white pinstriped suit and silk tie, Kykosawa didn't seem to be a businessman. He walked with confidence and grace, like a monarch in his castle. He smiled, but his eyes didn't seem to be part of the expression. Bolan noticed Kykosawa's companions sported bulges under their jackets, from the guns they carried in shoulder leather.

"Welcome, Mr. Trent," Kykosawa said with a bow. "It seems our timing is excellent. We all arrived here, in this room, at the same time. It must be fate. Yes?"

He spoke English very well and continued to display a professional smile, the type used by con men on every level throughout the world. Bolan had seen the same expression on the faces of street hustlers to candidates for president. Trent introduced him to Kykosawa and they exchanged bows.

"My associates aren't rude, but they don't speak English very well," Kykosawa explained. "I'm always glad to have a chance to practice the language myself. It keeps me from getting rusty. I believe we do have a lot to talk about. Come with us, please. We can discuss matters at the dinner table.''

"Fine, Kykosawa-*san*," Trent replied. *"Domo arigato."*

Bolan concealed his disappointment and frustration. The soldier wanted to examine the Kumo Shima office building, not spend time in a restaurant, spinning lies over sushi. However, Bolan had to play his role with conviction, and he couldn't think of any reason to insist they discuss business in the building.

Bolan and Trent followed the three Japanese. They emerged from the building and headed along the walkway. A long black limousine waited by the curb. They climbed into the back seat.

The limo rolled forward. Kykosawa and his companions sat opposite Bolan and Trent. The leader still acted as if the meeting made him happier than winning the lottery. His silent friends' faces seemed bland, but their eyes never left the two Americans.

"Do you like Italian food?" Kykosawa asked. "My cook makes an excellent lasagna."

"Your cook?" Trent asked with surprise.

"Yes. I have a house eighteen kilometers from the city. It is quiet, comfortable and far more pleasant to conduct business. Martial arts and raising funds for charity are not the same as arguing dcals about international trade or the stock exchange.''

A house, Bolan thought. Foley hadn't mentioned Kykosawa had a house. The background check the CIA ran was lacking critical information. Foley was either careless or something else was going on. The latter possibility made it difficult for Bolan to maintain a congenial front.

The limo made its way through the frantic traffic in Tokyo and reached an exit to the highway. The scent of saltwater drifted through the windows as they rode near the coast. Gulls hovered in the sky while the sun began to descend into the horizon.

"I'm glad to get away from the office today," Kykosawa stated. "There's too much going on. You might have heard about that unpleasant business that happened at our American branch."

"Yeah," Bolan replied. "Details are still vague. Sounds like one of the executives was giving drugs to people and involved with organized crime."

"Damn scandal," Kykosawa said with a sigh. "Investigators will be pouring over my records for days. Just a formality, of course. We had nothing to do with Robert Yong's misconduct, and at least he did everyone a favor by shooting himself. Hopefully, this will all blow over by the time your charity event begins. Tell me about it, Mr. Belasko."

Bolan began the cover story for his visit to Japan and the meeting with Kykosawa. The businessman seemed fascinated and listened with intense care. He nodded in agreement and asked few questions. But the man seemed too eager to go along with everything Bolan said. That formed a hard knot in the Executioner's stomach.

THE CAR TRAVELED a side road to a woodland area that seemed a world away from the busy, crowded city they had left. They approached the house. A sleek, split-level structure with wide picture windows and aluminum siding, only a pagoda-style roof expressed any

Asian influence on the otherwise Western design. Three vehicles were parked in front of the building as the limo came to a halt.

They emerged from the car. A stocky figure appeared at the door to the house. He was clad in a white *gi* martial-arts uniform. A black belt circled his waist, secured by a square knot near the navel. He bowed at Kykosawa and his guests.

"There is no need to remove your shoes," Kykosawa announced. "I have hardwood floors, not the traditional tatami mats."

Bolan felt as if he were about to step into a lion's den as he reached the threshold. The room within was a dojo with wood floors, white walls and a raised ceiling. Numerous martial-arts weapons and training devices decorated the walls, including a rack of *shinai* training swords for kendo. Half a dozen men dressed in *gi* uniforms stood at attention as Bolan and Trent entered. None wore a rank less than brown belt, third *dan*. They solemnly bowed at their guests.

Isolated from the other weapons, a pair of swords stood on display at the end of the room. The traditional *katana* long sword and *wakazashi* short sword of a samurai received a special place of honor. To the left of the swords, a sliding glass door stood open. A figure appeared to confirm that Bolan's sense of dread had been well-founded.

Major Choi, dressed in khakis and boots, stcppcd forward and raised a blue-black pistol. Bolan recognized the Beretta 93-R as well as the hard-faced North Korean who held it. Another man followed the major, an Uzi submachine gun clenched tightly in both hands.

"The dinner menu has been changed," Choi announced, "but that won't concern you two anyway. I doubt you have much of an appetite now."

Bolan met the Korean's mocking gaze. He glanced at Trent, who appeared bewildered to discover they had stepped into a trap. Kykosawa strolled past them to join Choi and the other gunman at the end of the hall. He appeared amused as he loosened his necktie.

"Don't look so surprised, Trent," he remarked. "Did you really think I'd welcome a mixed blood like you into my home? You're a walking insult to the Japanese people. The product of a white gaijin and a local slut. I find you even more disgusting than this American spy you brought us."

"I find an insult from a man like you more agreeable than praise," Trent replied in a firm voice.

"Speaking of American spies and lowlife," Bolan began, "is Foley here or doesn't he have the stomach to face someone he betrayed?"

"I'm here, Belasko," a voice announced.

The CIA case officer walked through the sliding doors. He held a Desert Eagle pistol in one hand and Trent's canvas case with the other. He dumped the bag on the floor and pointed the .44 Magnum pistol at Bolan's face.

"How'd you figure I was involved?" he asked. "Recognize your own guns? A lot of firepower you brought from home. Real impressive macho shit."

"I had a bad feeling about you from the start, Foley," Bolan stated. "You acted like you had never heard of Kykosawa or Kumo Shima before you were contacted as our liaison. The incident in Texas made international news, and it had already been linked to several bloody assassinations, including the murders of two U.S. congressmen. You didn't pay any attention to that? I knew you had to be acting. Maybe this was your way of being cool, but I was afraid you might be a damn traitor."

"Oh?" Foley asked with raised eyebrows. "What did I betray? You? Who the hell are you? A goddamn hired killer for the government? A mercenary working for Uncle Sam? You think you're a patriot, Belasko? You're just an attack dog that serves the corrupt interests of Washington."

"Capitalism," Choi said with a smile.

Foley stepped closer, the pistol still pointed at Bolan's face as the barrel swayed in his unsteady hand. The CIA man was accustomed to a desk job at the embassy and probably hadn't held a gun since the firing ranges at Langley, Virginia.

"Have you paid any attention to what our government has been doing?" Foley asked. "My brother was killed in Vietnam because we were supposed to be stopping the spread of communism. We let them take Laos and Cambodia. Then we made deals with the Russians and the Chinese. Global economy. It's all about making money and controlling people. As long as Washington has wealth and power, it doesn't care who it does business with."

"You're fed up with the system so you joined Kykosawa's scheme?" Bolan remarked.

"What the hell did you think you'd accomplish with that VR brainwashing and murders, Kykosawa?" he continued. "You just wanted to remove the competition so you could be top dog in the computer field?"

Kykosawa had removed his tie and suit jacket. He knelt by Trent's bag and examined some *shuriken* throwing stars. The sharp steel disks amused him as he glanced up at Bolan.

"The computer field is the most powerful in the world, Belasko," he explained. "Control it and you can control banking, communication, education. It's the way of the future. Your country is going to fall. America is headed for a total economic collapse. The entire Western economy will follow. When that happens, someone else will take command as the economic and political leader for the world."

"And that new power will be here in the Far East," Foley added. "Japan has had some economic ups and downs, but it hasn't dug itself a pit of debt so deep it'll never get out. That's what happened in the U.S.A. The government makes things worse and pretends it'll get better. They're not going to fix it. They screwed it up to begin with and just blame both parties instead of trying to do anything constructive. It's just a matter of time before it all falls down."

Kykosawa removed Trent's sword from the case. The plain black scabbard covered the long steel blade. A large square of black metal provided a hand guard at the hilt. Kykosawa shook his head and tossed the sword to the floor with contempt.

"This is really too absurd," he declared. "You think you're a ninja, Trent? No one told you they only exist in bad movies these days?"

"I am a ninja," Trent insisted. "You're a swordsman, Kykosawa. Get your fancy *katana* and I'll use my lowly ninja sword. Or are you only brave with bamboo and not with steel?"

"You're a fool," Kykosawa replied. "You think I'd agree to a duel when I have complete control of this situation? You're too stupid to live, Trent. That's why you'll die first."

He discovered the 9 mm Colt pistol in Trent's case.

Kykosawa called to a thug named Saito and tossed him the gun. The man aimed it at Trent. Bolan noticed Saito hadn't chambered a round. He hoped Trent was also aware of this.

"Your death will be long and painful," Kykosawa continued. "You don't matter, Trent. You don't know anything of value, so you can only be useful as an example of how terrible death can be. When Belasko sees you suffer and die slowly, he'll be happy to tell us everything he knows to get the reward of a swift and painless end."

"It's beginning to sound tempting just to avoid having to listen to you," Bolan commented. "You figure if you kill me nobody else will come for you?"

"We're not even sure what agency you work for," Kykosawa said, "but Mr. Foley tells me it must be very top secret and probably rather small. You'll be found without your head or hands. Lack of fingerprints and dental evidence will make identification difficult. You'll also have all these weapons of yours nearby. No doubt, they can't be traced to an owner. Everyone will assume you're an illegal gunrunner who crossed the Yakuza. The federal government in America won't want to acknowledge you because it would be a scandal."

"That's how Uncle Sam works," Foley added. "Only does what's in Washington's own best interest. We have the war against Iraq for the oil companies. We invade Panama for banking interests. The U.S. claims it loves democracy and hates communism, but Mainland China is one of our most favored trade partners. Forget about Tiananmen Square, the occupation of Tibet since 1951, human rights violations and slave labor. Uncle Sam has a good thing going with those Commie bastards and that's all that matters.''

"You don't mind North Korean Commie?" Bolan asked. "Major Choi is okay with you? The guy is such a Commie fanatic his own government would probably put him in front of a firing squad if he ever goes back there.''

"What the hell is he talking about?" Foley asked.

"Lies to confuse you," Choi said. "You know we're South Korean patriots. When the time comes, we'll support Japan for the construction of the new economic power to keep the Communists from taking advantage of the fall of the West.''

"You buy that, Foley?" Bolan asked. "Guess they managed to brainwash you without the use of drugs, hypnotic suggestion and virtual reality programs. Is that what you took from the wall safe at the Kumo Shima base in Dallas?''

Choi raised his eyebrows.

"Our VR programs are stored here," Kykosawa explained. "It's all in the next room. Programs for the subconscious to create illusions on demand, or our records on disk, everything you came for is all so close, Belasko. That doesn't matter because you won't live to see it now.''

"Maybe not," Bolan replied with a sigh, "but you and Choi won't last long as partners, either. You have different reasons for forming this agreement, and you're already getting in each other's way. I bet both of you are already planning how and when to kill the other. Learn some more about brainwashing and behavior modification to get rid of Choi. Steal, copy or reproduce the VR programs so Kykosawa won't be needed anymore. I wonder who'll stab who in the back first?''

"First, trying to get Foley to turn against us and now trying to get us to turn on each other," Choi said with a smile. "It won't work, Yankee pig."

"Neither will your insane plot," Trent declared.

"It'll work," Kykosawa insisted. "I admit we've had a setback, but we'll just change the name of the Kumo Shima products, reintroduce the line next year through a puppet company and continue where we left off.''

"Not when you hire idiots like Foley," Bolan said. "When we disappear my people are going to want to know what happened. The trail will lead straight to him.''

Foley glanced over a shoulder at Kykosawa. The Desert Eagle seemed to tremble a little more in his hand. Bolan surreptitiously stepped closer to the CIA man.

"Don't worry," Kykosawa assured Foley.

"You need to worry about him, Kykosawa," Bolan said. "Foley will break when they interrogate him. Look at this coward. He has a gun pointed at me, but he's the one shaking in his boots.''

"Shut up, you mother—"

Foley lashed out with the pistol, attempting to strike Bolan in the face with the barrel. The Executioner's hands rose swiftly to catch the fist around the Desert Eagle. He bent Foley's wrist and shoved the pistol as the agent pulled the trigger in panicked desperation. The big gun roared within the confines of the dojo. The last thing Foley saw was the muzzle-flash explode in his face.

Bolan yanked the weapon from Foley's hand as his

body began to sag, part of his head reduced to crimson-gray pulp from the .44 Magnum round that pierced his skull. The Executioner gripped the Eagle in both hands and dropped to a kneeling stance. The enemy appeared stunned, caught off guard by the unexpected action and the thunderous roar of the big pistol. None was really accustomed to combat, and Bolan had to make the most of the mere seconds required for them to recover from the shock.

Choi swung the Beretta toward Bolan as the Eagle bellowed again. A .44 Magnum slug tore into the Korean's solar plexus and exited between his shoulder blades. The impact hurled Choi almost two yards, sending him crashing to the floor, his chest cavity filling with blood and his spine split in two.

The guard with the Uzi raised the submachine gun, putting the stock to his shoulder. Had he fired from the hip, he might have taken out the Executioner. Bolan didn't hesitate as he swung his pistol from target to target, squeezing the trigger. Another .44 round hit the submachine gunner under the left eye, cracking the socket and slicing into his brain. Skull fragments and blood spewed from the back of the man's head.

With the three immediate threats taken out, Bolan scanned the room. Trent had taken advantage of the distraction to disarm the gunman who threatened him with the Colt pistol. A hard kick sent the weapon from the guy's grasp, and Trent followed with a side of the hand stroke to his opponent's throat. The thug staggered backward, hands clasped to his crushed windpipe. Saito's knees buckled and he dropped to the floor.

Kykosawa dived to the floor to avoid the flying bullets, but he didn't produce a weapon to return fire. Apparently, he wasn't familiar with guns and didn't carry one. The Tigers of Business, clad in *gi* attire, backed up to the walls. Unarmed, they weren't eager to rush the soldier with the big steel pistol. A shape appeared at the door. Bolan recognized one of Kykosawa's bodyguards and saw the guy draw a Nambu pistol from his jacket.

Bolan nailed the hood with a .44 Magnum slug to the chest. The force of the projectile propelled the gunman backward, across the threshold and outside. One of the *gi*-clad characters rushed forward to scoop up the fallen Colt pistol. Bolan shot him in the chest before he could use the weapon. Aware he might need more firepower, Bolan switched the Desert Eagle to his left hand and pried the Uzi SMG from the grasp of the corpse that held it.

Trent reached for the closest weapon—his ninja sword. He glimpsed movement along the wall and saw one hoodlum had decided to grab the martial-arts weapons from the walls. A bold opponent raised a *shinai* overhead and charged as Trent drew his sword.

The ninja blade rose to meet the enemy attack. Split bamboo met sharp steel with the expected result. The startled thug stared at the stump that remained of his training sword. Trent followed with a ruthless sword stroke that sliced the guy's face from the crown of his head to the middle of his nose.

Another opponent attacked with a *sai* in each fist. A metal truncheon with a long center blade and two shorter tines, a *sai* was an efficient weapon in the right hands. If the opponent could trap Trent's sword between the shaft and tine of one *sai,* he could strike or thrust with the pointed blade of the other. The American ninja had to guess what tactic the *sai* fighter would employ.

The hoodlum tried to snare Trent's blade with a *sai*, ready to counterstrike with the other. However, Trent's blade didn't move where he expected. The ninja suddenly stepped right and completed the actual sword stroke. Sharp steel caught the man above the fist holding the *sai* to chop into the man's wrist. The thug screamed as he stared down at his own hand on the floor, the *sai* still clenched in the fingers. Blood gushed from the stump that was left of his arm. Trent finished by striking him in the temple with the sword handle to silence him.

Trent saw movement out of the corner of his eye. An attacker attempted to deliver a blow from behind with a *shinai*. Trent swung his sword to meet the attack, the flat of his blade striking the bamboo weapon to block and deflect it. The American saw the surprised and alarmed expression on the face of his opponent as he slashed the sword in a diagonal stroke.

Steel flashed beneath the chin of the *shinai*-wielding hood. Blood flowed from the man's slit throat to dye the white *gi* jacket scarlet. The man stumbled, dropped his bamboo weapon and crumpled to the floor.

TWO FIGURES ARMED with pistols entered through the sliding glass door. Mack Bolan had expected the thugs outside to attempt an attack from that direction after he took out the gunman who came through the front door. The Executioner pointed his Uzi at the pair, squeezed the trigger and sprayed the gunners with a lethal salvo of 9 mm slugs.

Glass shattered and the bullet-torn bodies of the Kumo Shima goons toppled across the threshold. Bolan scanned the dojo, Uzi clenched in one fist, its stock firmly braced on his hip, and the Desert Eagle held in the other hand. He noticed Trent in combat with the enemy, but the American ninja didn't appear to need any help as he chopped down opponents with his long blade.

A *gi*-clad thug screamed a battle cry and charged Bolan with a nunchaku in hand. He held one wood stick in a fist as the second whirled in a rapid set of figure-eight cuts in the air, attached by a short chain at the center. The weapon could be lethal at close quarters, but Bolan didn't intend to let the man gain that advantage.

The Desert Eagle bellowed once more and a .44 round lifted the attacker off his feet and dumped him on the floor. The nunchaku clattered on the hardwood surface as the hoodlum's body slid toward the front doorway. A Kumo Shima killer chose that moment to enter, a cut-down shotgun in his fists. He glanced down at the slain figure, distracted and startled to see a dead comrade by his feet.

Bolan didn't give him a chance to recover. The Executioner blasted the shotgunner with a trio of Uzi projectiles, splitting the guy's breastbone and puncturing the hollow of his throat. A blur of motion warned Bolan danger approached, and he swung the Uzi to his right.

A long shaft of steel struck the frame of his SMG. Kykosawa faced the Executioner, the samurai *katana* clenched in both fists, *wakazashi* short sword thrust in his belt. The Kumo Shima leader shoved with the long blade to push the Uzi aside as he swung a roundhouse karate kick to Bolan's right arm.

The combination of the pressure by the sword and the kick forced the Executioner to release the Uzi. Metal struck the floor, and the subgun skidded out of reach. Bolan jumped back as Kykosawa raised the *ka-*

tana. The soldier pointed the Desert Eagle at the enemy and squeezed the trigger. A dull click announced the weapon was out of ammo.

Kykosawa hesitated when he saw the muzzle threaten him, but smiled with confidence to discover the fearsome Desert Eagle was empty. Bolan suddenly flicked his wrist and hurled the big steel pistol at the swordsman's face. Kykosawa ducked and raised the hilt of his sword to parry the airborne handgun. The Executioner hadn't expected to hit his opponent with the pistol. He only hoped to distract Kykosawa for a split second to retreat from the range of the long samurai blade.

Bolan raced to the nearest wall and the rack of stick weapons displayed there. He had little time to make a selection and grabbed a shaft of rock maple from the rack, gripping the stave with both hands. The pole measured about one yard long, the wood thick and solid. Bolan had handled such stick weapons before. It was known as a *hanbo*, a favorite among bo jitsu martial artists.

"You think that will help you, Belasko?" Kykosawa asked with an amused smile. "You're a fool and about to become a dead one."

Bolan didn't respond. Kykosawa slowly advanced, *katana* held forward, its sharp tip at eye level, its deadly edge directed toward the American. Bolan realized a blade that could cut into the steel frame of an Uzi could easily chop the stick in two or slice off an arm, leg or head with a single stroke.

Kykosawa's shoulders shifted to the right and signaled the direction of his attack. Steel flashed. Bolan swung the *hanbo* and slammed it across the flat of the *katana* blade. Kykosawa shuffled in a semicircle and delivered another sword stroke aimed at Bolan's neck.

The Executioner also moved in a circular pattern away from the attack and brought the shaft down hard across the spine of Kykosawa's weapon. The blow deflected the attack, and Bolan quickly thrust the end of his *hanbo* under Kykosawa's arm. He jammed the stick against the hilt of the sword between his opponent's fists and shoved hard. Bolan turned with the push to increase the force behind the move. Combined with Kykosawa's own momentum, the tactic hurled the swordsman off balance and sent him forward into the wall.

The Kumo Shima mastermind slammed into the surface and turned to face Bolan. The Executioner chopped the hardwood shaft across his adversary's wrists and struck the *katana* from Kykosawa's grasp. The sword fell to the floor at the Japanese's feet, and Bolan immediately pushed his advantage with a hard thrust under his enemy's rib cage. The *hanbo* jabbed Kykosawa with painful force and drove the breath from his lungs.

Bolan whipped the wood pole across the side of Kykosawa's knee, and the leg folded. He slid along the wall, trying to remain on his feet and gain some distance from Bolan. The Executioner held the *hanbo* in one hand and reached down with the other to grasp the hilt of the fallen *katana*. Kykosawa hissed with rage and frustration as he pushed away from the wall and drew the *wakazashi* from his belt.

He charged, the short sword clenched in both hands. Bolan raised the *katana* and pointed it at Kykosawa's torso. The Kumo Shima leader literally ran into the long blade before he could get close enough to attempt a *wakazashi* stroke. Bolan wasn't certain if Kykosawa had done this by accident or design, aware the battle was lost and eager to end it.

Either way, the result was the same. The sharp slanted point of the *katana* pierced Kykosawa's chest, penetrating muscle and bone to puncture the man's heart. A bloodied finger of steel burst from Kykosawa's back near the left shoulder blade. Bolan pushed the sword and shoved the enemy ringleader into the wall. Kykosawa slid to the floor as his corpse twitched once and curled around the long blade jammed into his lifeless flesh.

"This is the last time I'm doing this," John Trent declared. "I thought I'd have a heart attack before anyone could get a chance to kill me."

The American ninja approached, bloodstained sword in one hand and the 9 mm Colt pistol in the other. Mack Bolan located his Beretta 93-R near the corpse of Major Choi, but he didn't need it. All the Kumo Shima enemies were dead.

"You're still alive, John," Bolan said. "The guys who tried to kill us aren't. Take a deep breath and appreciate the fact you can still do so."

"I smell blood, gunpowder and death," Trent replied. "Is it over?"

"It's over," Bolan assured him. "We still have to find Kykosawa's virtual reality program and his records, but he even told us where to look. We'll get the stuff, borrow one of the cars outside and head back to Tokyo. I'll call the embassy and have them arrange a flight back for us. Also I'm going to tell them to screen all CIA contacts more carefully in future. I don't want to find myself working with another Judas like Foley."

Trent glanced at the body of Kykosawa and said,

"I'll never understand men like him. Kykosawa was brilliant. He had wealth, power and prestige. Why wasn't that enough?"

"Some people never have enough," the Executioner replied. "That's why they're miserable and they bring misery to others. They never get what they want and sooner or later they end up like this."

"Everybody dies, Belasko," Trent commented. "Even you will one day."

"Yeah," Mack Bolan agreed. "But not today."

In the Deathlands, power is the ultimate weapon....

JAMES AXLER

DEATH LANDS®

Gemini Rising

Ryan Cawdor comes home to West Virginia and his nephew Nathan, to whom Cawdor had entrusted the Cawdor barony. Waiting for Cawdor are two of his oldest enemies, ready to overtake the barony and the Cawdor name.

Unable to help an ailing Krysty Wroth, Cawdor must face this challenge to the future of the East Coast baronies on his own.

Book 1 in the Baronies Trilogy, three books that chronicle the strange attempts to unify the East Coast baronies—a bid for power in the midst of anarchy....